"Do you su... it in one... take more... once?..."

Drake choked on his hamburger and coughed. His dark-hued complexion turned a dusky shade of red.

Aria patted him on the back. "Are you all right?"

"Yes. Fine." With his eyes springing tears, he downed half a glass of milk, then drew a deep breath.

"So, what do you think? Will once be enough?"

"If the timing's right, that's all it takes."

Aria puzzled over that as she ate another oyster. She knew little about the mating cycle of human females. Failure was a risk she didn't dare take. Certainly trying extra hard would not be an onerous burden, but rather a pleasurable one.

Looking across the table, she smiled brightly. "I think we ought to do it as many times as possible between now and tomorrow morning. That way we'll be sure."

Drake started coughing again, so hard this time, he had to get up and leave the room. Aria sincerely hoped he wasn't coming down with something. A delay at this late date, due to his incapacity, could spell disaster for her.

Dear Reader,

Once upon a time we were little girls dreaming of handsome princes on white chargers, of fairy godmothers who'd made us into beautiful princesses and of mountain castles where we'd live happily ever after.

Now that we're all grown up, we can recapture those dreams in a brand-new miniseries, Once Upon a Kiss. It features stories based on some of the world's best-loved fairy tales.

Charlotte Maclay continues the series with the retelling of the classic fairy tale *The Little Mermaid*, one of my personal favorites.

Be sure to read all six of these wonderful fairy-tale romances, coming to you only from American Romance!

Once Upon a Kiss—at the heart of every little girl's dreams...and every woman's fantasy....

Happy reading!

Debra Matteucci
Senior Editor & Editorial Coordinator
Harlequin
300 E. 42nd St.
New York, NY 10017

Charlotte Maclay

CATCHING A DADDY

Harlequin Books

TORONTO • NEW YORK • LONDON
AMSTERDAM • PARIS • SYDNEY • HAMBURG
STOCKHOLM • ATHENS • TOKYO • MILAN
MADRID • WARSAW • BUDAPEST • AUCKLAND

Special thanks to Mindy and Joan—you know how much you mean to me—and the ladies of the Vancouver RWA chapter for helping me find mermaids in beautiful British Columbia. Bet you didn't know she'd turn out like this! And to Diane, whose idea made it all work.

ISBN 0-373-16709-1

CATCHING A DADDY

Chapter One

"How come you gots a tail?"

Startled, Aria swirled around in the chill water of the sheltered cove and looked up at the youngster standing on the dock. Curious dark brown eyes questioned her. No more than a small-fry—a child of perhaps six years—Aria recognized he posed no threat to her.

"Because I am a mermaid," she answered with a smile. Lifting her tail, she slapped the water and sent an airy splash up over the dock.

Hopping out of the way, he giggled. "Do you like having a tail?"

"It's quite useful for swimming. Do you like to swim?"

"Sure, but my dad only lets me swim in the summer. He says it's too cold now."

Shivering, she thrust a sideways stroke with her tail and glided around in a circle. "Your father is right. Winter will soon be here." With winter's arrival the water temperature would drop even further along the coastal waters that swept the western edge of the great continent. Soon lethargy would set in, and Aria would have no hope of discovering the school of merpeople she'd been searching for since her banishment from her place of birth. In these northern waters, she might not survive until the spring came, bringing warmth, renewed energy and the ability to escape hungry predators.

Somehow she must have taken a wrong turn on her journey, or the currents had carried her far off course. Friendly otters and harbor seals she'd met along the way had assured her of other mermaids living in this vicinity. But there'd been no sign. None at all.

Lonely fear rippled through her. Life alone was the cruelest punishment to which Aria's stepmother could have condemned her. Oceana must be gloating over her victory.

The youngster walked along a narrow board at the edge of the dock, carefully placing one foot in front of the other, his arms outstretched for balance. He wore a heavy brown jacket that hung open; his hair was a shade almost as dark as the depths of the ocean. "My dad's a fisherman."

Aria's gaze shot to the boat tied up near the child. "Does he use nets?" Gill nets like the one which had trapped and ultimately killed her father?

"Naw. He uses a fishin' pole. A big one 'cause he catches real big fish." He teetered precariously on the narrow strip of wood before regaining his balance. "I'm gonna be a fisherman when I grow up."

"The sea can be a dangerous place."

"I'm not scared." As if to emphasize his youthful bravado, he spun around on one foot. His balance faltered. Arms waving, he tried to find solid purchase for his feet and failed.

Just as the boy tumbled headlong into the water, a man shouted a warning from the structure that stood at the far end of the dock. "Ma...thew!"

Aria scooped up the youngster before he'd sunk more than a few inches below the water's surface. Tail whipping back and forth to lift her as high as possible, she hefted the child back onto the dock.

Matthew sputtered and coughed, his eyes wide with surprise and amazement to find himself back on the dock so quickly.

"You're all right, small-fry," Aria soothed in a lilting voice.

The man sprinting down the dock toward them shouted again. "Matt!"

From Aria's perspective, he was a huge human, his hair as wild and dark as the boy's, his eyebrows pulling taut, like two black mountains determined to challenge each other in battle, peaking above the straight ridge of his nose.

Terrified, she slipped below the surface of the water. Human children were usually accepting of a mermaid, but adult males were as likely to be aggressive as cordial. Admittedly, the reputation of mermaids for luring sailors to their deaths was well founded. Aria's own stepmother was particularly adept at the evil trick. In contrast, Aria found humans strangely intriguing and under no circumstances would she want to harm one.

She swam deeper into the waters of the sheltered cove. Even here she could feel the tug of the current, pulling her north. The surface shifted above her. A storm was brewing, racing toward her from frigid arctic waters. If she was to find a school of merpeople, she needed to swim south again. But she could feel the cold water sapping her strength. The current was too powerful to fight and, with the pull of the tide, she felt her hopes ebbing away.

Soon there would be a full moon.

If she came out of the water when the moon was at its peak, it might be her salvation. Or her sentence to a fate far worse than death. For in the full moon, a mermaid stranded on land took the form of a human. When the moon returned to its zenith in the next cycle, the mermaid must slip back into the sea or risk becoming a rotting banquet for seagulls. The only other choice was to become pregnant with the milt of a human male.

Aria shuddered.

She had no idea how humans mated, though she had once observed peculiar antics going on between a male and female on a beach somewhere to the south. At this point, her decided preference would be to find a school of merpeople who would welcome her.

Flipping onto her back, she glanced up through the water to the dark clouds that were scudding by overhead. A swell lifted her toward the surface and dropped her past a baby sea perch, who interrupted his grazing around a piling to gaze at her curiously. It was going to be a severe storm, she realized. And though she'd found a sheltered cove, she still might not be out of harm's way.

Drake Hart lunged toward his son and lifted him into his arms. "Matt! Haven't I told you a thousand times to be careful out here? What the heck happened?"

"I s-s-slipped. I didn't m-m-mean to."

Hugging his son tight, Drake took a deep breath and tried to swallow the fear that had crowded in his throat. He hadn't meant to yell at the boy. It always made Matt's stuttering worse when he got mad at him. But when he'd seen the boy tumbling into the water, Drake had been frantic.

The image repeated itself in Drake's mind to a renewed surge of terror. His son—

Like looking at a video replay, he froze the picture on a single frame.

"Hey, how'd you get back on the dock so fast?"

"The m-m-mermaid p-p-put me back."

"The mermaid?"

Matt nodded. His eyes were wide with a combination of excitement and surprise.

Suppressing a reprimand about making up wild tales, Drake said, "It's okay, son. Let's get you back home and out of these wet clothes. I don't want you catching cold." He hefted the boy around to his back to carry him piggyback style. Matt latched on tight around Drake's neck, making the lump in Drake's throat swell again with a big dose of love.

"She had a t-tail."

"Sure. And you wanted to go swimming with her, right?"

"It's too c-cold."

"You bet it is." The first big storm of the season was bearing down on the British Columbia coast, and they were in for a couple of cold, wet days. He'd already lashed his twenty-foot Boston Whaler securely to the dock and pulled all the rental skiffs out of the water. There'd be no fishing charters until after the storm blew past, and darn few visitors to the Hart's Cove Marina or rental cabins.

"How come the m-mermaid doesn't get cold in the water?" Matt asked.

"I don't know, son. Maybe it's because you've been watching too many cartoons on television." And creating even wilder stories on his own.

"Uh-uh."

The dock shifted under Drake's footsteps, a comfortable rocking motion. He'd been born with sea legs, he mused, an inheritance from both his father and grandfather. He hoped to pass on the same legacy to his son.

Unfortunately, his former wife hadn't shared his love for a life of relative solitude among the nooks and crannies of the northern gulf islands. After giving him a wonderful son, she'd been far more interested in pursuing the fast lane with a hippie guitar player, who was supposedly going to make it big in the recording business. In her case, the fast lane turned into a dead end on a highway near Seattle.

Thank God she hadn't taken Matt with her. She'd claimed that a one-year-old son would be an inconvenience in her new life.

He wasn't an inconvenience for Drake. Not even close, he thought with an abundance of parental pride, though there were definitely moments when he wasn't sure he was cut out to be both mom and dad. But most days he managed. Somehow.

And no way would he ever put himself in a spot again where a woman could mess up his head and tie his heart in sailor knots, then walk away. It simply wouldn't happen.

He pushed open the door of their home, a houseboat parked at the edge of the dock, and lowered his son to the floor.

"Okay, little chip, down you go."

"How c-come you call me 'little chip'?"

Kneeling, he helped Matt take off his soggy jacket. It was getting too small for the boy, and that meant a trip to the general store was due. "'Cause you're a chip off the ol' block. That's me."

"She called me 'small fry.'"

"Who did?"

"The m-mermaid."

"Yeah, well, that's a pretty good name, too." He ruffled his son's dark hair, as straight and thick as his own. "Go get changed and stick the wet stuff in the dryer. We've got macaroni and cheese for dinner."

"Again?" the boy complained.

"Hey, it's one of your favorites."

Matt pulled a petulant face. "I guess."

THE RAIN STARTED sometime in the night and built in intensity during the following day. Wind buffeted the cove, cutting loose logs from logging rafts and driving them onto the shore to join a bone yard of flotsam.

Drake puttered at jobs that required him to be outside as little as possible—overhauling the innards of a Evinrude engine, mending gear and cleaning out the big freezer his clients used to save their catch for later shipment to the States.

By evening the storm had hit its peak. He put Matt to bed, then paced the floor. His restlessness went well beyond irritation with the weather. Its source was far more deep-seated, though Drake was reluctant to give it a name.

He peered out the window into the driving storm. A flat rock marked the divide between his cove and the broader waters of the strait. Waves lifted over the shelf, pouring back in on themselves as a new surge swept across the granite outcropping.

Squinting, he thought he saw something on that rock. A beached harbor seal, maybe. Though he hated to see any injured animal, he didn't have all that much sympathy for a marine competitor that ate the catch he depended upon for his livelihood.

As he watched, the clouds parted momentarily. A

full moon sent a shaft of light right toward the table rock.

Drake's breath caught. He had the distinct impression the creature on that rock was a person.

A woman.

He shook his head. What the hell would a woman be doing stranded on a rock at the entrance to Hart's Cove?

The figure moved and so did Drake.

Pulling on his slicker and slamming on his all-weather hat, hc ran for the boat tied at the dock, counting on the powerful outboard engine to give him all the control he needed in the heavy seas. The rain slapped at his face like an angry woman.

Instantly his fingers wcrc so cold that he fumbled as he released the aft line, then struggled to cast off the bow. He jumped on board. Even here in the sheltered cove, the waves pitched the boat from side to side, bashing it against the dock before he could get the motor started.

The clouds closed in on themselves. Roiling black billows crossed the sky, sending the moon into hiding again. It didn't matter. Drake knew where the marker rock was. He'd navigated around it for most of his thirty years and could have found—or avoided—the outcropping in his sleep. This time he intended to rescue whatever creature had been tossed there by the fury of the sea.

He maneuvered with care. In spite of the normally benign appearance of these waters, tides and currents could make them treacherous. A storm compounded the problem.

The two hundred horses, throbbing powerfully through the engine, responded with almost psychic precision to his commands. He came alongside the rock.

He'd been right.

A woman. With the longest, most beautifully shaped legs he'd ever seen. And she was naked, screened only by a froth of waist-length hair the shade of silver moonbeams tangling together.

"Oh, man..." he mumbled, uttering a curse. What cruise ship had she fallen off? And what in the hell kind of wild party had she been attending?

Using a pole, he steadied the boat long enough so he could reach over the gunnel and haul the woman aboard. She was cold—icy cold—but her skin was like pure satin, sleek and sexy and reminding Drake of needs he'd set aside years ago.

He wasn't going to look. Not at the swell of her breast that pressed against his chest. Not at the curve of her hip that rested right at his belt buckle as he carried her into the boat's cabin and placed her on the narrow bunk—a bunk wide enough that several of his clients had enjoyed the intimate company of their wives or lady friends there while taking a break from fishing.

He decided he was gonna be a saint and not even sneak a peak as he wrapped her in a blanket.

In your dreams—

No man could ignore a dream that good.

The hull scraped against the rock. Drake cursed again and headed for the wheel. He had to get out of there before the storm turned his boat into uninsured toothpicks.

Applying full throttle, he wheeled the boat on its tail and hauled back toward the dock. Wind and waves chased ahead of the prow, driving him back into the cove.

In spite of the bloody gash he'd seen on the woman's forehead, he was pretty sure she was still alive. He meant to make sure she didn't die on his watch.

He secured the boat, double-checked the lines and carried the woman into the houseboat. Not knowing what else to do with her, he laid her on the tumble of sheets and blankets on his unmade bed. She looked good there. Like she belonged.

And he knew he shouldn't be thinking like that.

As he covered her, she hummed a sigh that sounded as sweet as a summer sea stroking a sandy beach. She stirred restlessly and a smile tugged at the corners of full, sensual lips. Her eyes blinked open—sea green and unfocused.

"It's okay, lady. You've had an accident."

Aria heard the voice—deep and masculine and strangely disturbing. Moving awkwardly, she searched for the source. Then, with stunning clarity, she realized—

She sat bolt upright. "Legs!"

"What's wrong? Are your legs hurt?"

Her gaze snapped up to the human male who was

standing close to her. Threateningly close. "No. I
don't think so." Her attention shifted downward, to
the mound the covers concealed. Tossing back the
blankets, she stared at her two new appendages.
"Legs," she muttered, incredulous. She wiggled her
toes, twisted her ankles, flexed her knees. To her
dismay, all the parts appeared to be in perfect working order. How had she been so careless as to leave
the water on a night with a full moon? Even a mer-
baby knew better than that!

"Miss, er, ah…"

She looked again at the man. The boy's father,
she realized. At this distance he seemed a little less
intimidating than he had on the dock, though no less
dangerous. Except now he was looking at her very
strangely, the muscles in his throat working rapidly
up and down as he swallowed two or three times in
succession.

Odd behavior, she mused.

"Is there something troubling you?" she asked.
Her skin began to flush under his intense scrutiny.

"You, ah…don't have any clothes on." His gaze
still riveted on her, he made a vague gesture.

"Clothes?" Of course not. Why would he think
a mermaid needed clothes?

Except she wasn't a mermaid any longer. She
was a human—temporarily, at least. That reality
slammed into her like an oversize wave and knocked
her off her equilibrium. She groaned and closed her
eyes.

"You'd better take it easy a minute." Strong,

masculine hands eased her back to the pillow, his touch sending a strangely electric thrill through her. He pulled the covers back into place and stepped away so quickly, she wondered if he had experienced the same powerful current. "You've got a nasty cut on your head. I'll, ah, get some antiseptic to clean it and a bandage. You've probably got the world's worse headache about now." He fled the room in hurried strides.

Aria's head did hurt, but less from the injury than from her impossible situation. How could she find a school of merpeople to join if she couldn't swim? And humans, she knew, weren't very good at swimming or breathing underwater. A serious limitation in her view.

In another month, winter would be at gale force at this latitude and she would never succeed in her quest. Unless the merpeople were very close. And this human male knew how to find them.

He returned, setting his supplies on the table beside her.

"This is likely to hurt some," he said gruffly. Working with care, he daubed the cut with a dampened cloth.

She sucked in a quick breath at the stinging pain.

"Sorry."

"It's all right." Her eyes watered and she blinked.

As he continued to work, she studied him beneath half-lowered lids. He appeared to be an excellent specimen—broad shoulders, muscular arms and long, powerful legs. His face was a bit ragged with whiskers, as rough appearing as black coral. She flinched at the mere thought of those whiskers brushing against her sensitive flesh. But he did have nice eyes, a warm brown that sparked with keen alertness, and apparently he had rescued her when she'd floundered. A generous man who was also gentle.

He finished his ministrations by applying a bandage, then stepped back as if to admire his handiwork. "Look, is there somebody I can call for you? To let them know you're okay."

A frown pulled the adhesive tight on her forehead. "I don't think so."

"You fall off a ship or something?"

"A ship? No, nothing like that."

He looked at her in a puzzled way. "Do you know your name?"

"Of course." She smiled at him. Humans asked the oddest questions. "It's Aria."

He cocked his head. "Just the one name?"

"One is all I have ever needed."

His brows peaked together like two opposing prongs of Neptune's fork. "I suppose that means you're a rock singer or something."

"Why, yes, I love to sing," she admitted happily, "and I often sit on rocks while I practice. How did you know?"

Drake tunneled his fingers through his hair. Maybe if this Aria person had some clothes on he'd be able to think more clearly. He knew damn well she was a singer. She had the most melodic speaking voice he'd ever heard. And who else besides an entertainer would be so totally unconcerned about being naked as the day she was born?

Shoot, he should have left her out there on that rock.

And if it hadn't been for the sight of that beautiful body, a vision he would always remember if he lived to be a hundred, her impish green eyes would have gotten to him. He had the oddest feeling she was constantly on the verge of laughter. Though he fought the sensation, down deep in his gut he wanted to join in the fun.

"I'm going to find you something to wear," he said more harshly than he had intended.

"I suppose that would be appropriate."

She had that damn straight. "Are you hungry?"

"A little. With the storm... The rough weather makes it difficult to graze—ah, eat."

"Great. I'll heat up some leftover macaroni. Matt will be glad to have somebody finish it up for us." He turned to leave, then glanced back over his shoulder. A mistake. She'd sat up again and the damn blanket had slipped down to her waist. Her breasts were each a perfect handful, her nipples rosy and puckered from the cold. Gritting his teeth, he throttled back his instinctive reaction. "By the way, I'm Drake Hart. Two names. And for the moment, you're at Hart's Cove on Oyster Island. When the storm passes, I'll take you wherever you want to go."

HE BROUGHT HER a heavy shirt that was several sizes too large, the shoulders hanging almost to her elbows, the hem very nearly reaching her knees. Though a bit scratchy on her sensitive skin, it was comfortably warm, and she rolled up the sleeves so they wouldn't droop like broken flippers. The shorts he provided were equally big, and she had to tie a knot at the waist for fear they would slip off.

Humans, Aria realized, were an overly modest species. She'd never experienced any shame about her body as a mermaid and felt no such emotion now in her human form.

Admittedly, her new legs were a bit hard to manage and made her so tall she could hardly believe how high she was above about the floor—higher than the most vigorous whipping of her tail had ever allowed her to rise above the sea. She balanced precariously on one leg, then lowered the second foot to the floor. She tottered, unsure of what to do next, then steadied herself with one hand on the wall. Taking a deep breath, she wiggled up onto her toes and hopped forward.

No, that wasn't right, she thought, barely regaining her balance before she fell in a heap. She'd seen humans walk, and they definitely didn't leap around like a fish flopping out of the water.

Trying again, she took a mincing step, wobbled fiercely and grabbed a handful of the fabric dangling around the window. Though not at all graceful, she managed several steps on the next try, before her loss of equilibrium brought her to her knees with a soft thud.

She sighed.

With fresh insight, she realized how truly difficult it must be for a drunken sailor to maneuver safely across the deck of a ship. Simply standing upright on two legs was a giddy and challenging experience.

Once she acquired some mastery over her new legs, she toured the room. Even as a child she'd been curious about humans, often spying on them in their homes near the beach or in their boats that sailed past. But never before had she been so close. Still, she'd gained enough knowledge to understand much of what she was seeing and hearing.

The bed where Drake had placed her was quite generous in size. Only one other piece of furniture was in the room, and on the top of that was a grinning picture of Matt when he'd been little more than a baby. In spite of the child's smile, Aria sensed loneliness in the room, almost as distressing to her emotions as the lingering scent of diesel fuel polluting fresh sea air was to her sense of smell.

Somewhere in her heart she felt the echo of the same painful feeling deep inside herself.

Using a comb she found next to the boy's picture, she worked the tangles from her hair as she might have used the spines of a sea urchin. Finally she was ready to go in search of Drake.

HE DIDN'T NEED THIS.

Aria looked sexier in his old wool shirt than she

had stark naked. Which was a darn hard act to follow.

Drake began to sweat. Other parts of his anatomy appeared particularly alert to the graceful way she walked, the sway of her hips, that mass of long hair he wanted to feel draped over him.

He swallowed hard. She'd be out of here soon. He'd see to that.

"You ready to eat?" he asked. He gestured toward a chair at the small table where he and Matt usually ate their meals.

"Yes, thank you." She glided into her place with no more effort than a boat sailing over smooth water. "Are you eating, too?" Her shirt gaped open, revealing—

Drake headed for the refrigerator. "No, I'll just have a beer." The fact was, he ought to have his head examined. A call to 911 to get her out of here would be the smartest thing he could do. Except in this storm he doubted any emergency services could make it to Hart's Cove, either by land or sea. The wind was still howling around the houseboat, and waves lifted the dock at erratic intervals, making the boards groan. The rain had no doubt turned the single dirt road that ran the length of the island into a quagmire of mud. They'd all be stuck here until the storm passed.

Aria examined the food he placed in front of her with considerable trepidation. Little white sea worm tubes lay there covered in a yellow sauce.

"I don't think I'm hungry after all," she said weakly.

"You don't like macaroni?"

"It's fine, I'm sure." Her stomach churned. She didn't dare anger this human male, not if she hoped to garner his help in finding merpeople. She took a bite. Letting the tube slide down her throat, she forced a smile. Surely she'd tasted worse.

"You want something to drink?"

"Water, I think." She toyed with her fork, shoving the slippery macaroni tubes around the plate in the hope he wouldn't realize she wasn't really eating them.

At the sink he filled a glass container with water, then placed it in front of her. "So tell me, if you didn't fall off a boat, how did you get on that rock where I found you?"

"I'm not sure." Nor did she think he would be sympathetic if she told him she'd been searching for fellow mermaids. Assuming he believed her, a human male was not likely to be pleased with the prospect of a mermaid in his house.

"You don't remember?"

"Not exactly. Maybe it's the bump on my head." She took a sip of water. Decidedly bland, she thought. "Do you have any salt?"

"Sure." He shoved a small container across the table.

She sprinkled salt into the water, tasted it again and smiled.

Oh, dear, she'd obviously made a serious error.

His dramatic eyebrows had leaped upward in surprise.

"Do you always put salt in your drinking water?"

Her smile faltered as she searched for a way to cover her mistake. "I like to drink salt water when I'm eating macaroni. You should try it sometime." She forked a yellow-coated tube worm into her mouth and swallowed it.

From the corner of her eye, she spotted an orange, striped land animal padding across the room. Disconcerted, she watched as the creature circled her curiously and began sniffing at her legs.

"That's Buffy, my son's cat," Drake said. "She won't hurt you."

She moved her legs out of the way, but the cat persisted in her exploration, rubbing against her.

"The doctor said kids who stutter often talk to animals better than they do to people. So when this stray showed up, I told Matt he could keep her."

"Your son stutters?" She hadn't noticed that when she'd talked with the boy on the dock. But perhaps that was because he'd known she was a mermaid.

"Yeah. The doc is pretty sure he'll outgrow it. Most kids do if you don't make a big deal out of it. You'll meet Matt in the morning."

"I'll look forward to that." She tried to shoo the cat away with a gentle shove of her leg, but the animal stubbornly continued to sniff at her. Her nose was damp and cold; her whiskers tickled where they brushed against Aria's bare leg.

"You should be flattered. Buffy doesn't usually take to strangers. Unless they're cleaning fish on the dock. Then she's anybody's friend."

She shuddered as though a knife was about to slice into her gullet. "Yes, well, I guess I have a way with animals." More typically with otters and seals and an occasional baby whale, rather than with curious cats.

Drake took a swig of beer from the bottle. He was having real trouble calibrating his unexpected dinner guest. This was one distracting lady the storm had swept up onto his shore. Sexy and evasive, he decided. A disturbing combination. She had a secret she wasn't about to let him in on, and that bugged him.

Maybe in the morning she'd be a little more forthcoming. If not, he'd take her into the island village and have a private chat with the local police.

Beautiful women didn't simply fall off a boat— or get dumped overboard—without someone missing them. It didn't make any sense that she had been swimming around out there on her own. Naked.

Or that the nasty, but relatively minor, cut on her head had given her amnesia.

So where the heck had she come from?

Chapter Two

"You won't tell your daddy, will you?"

"Uh-uh. But won't he see your tail?"

"I don't have a tail at the moment." To her everlasting regret, Aria noted. "I've got legs."

Matt's gaze shifted to the limbs in question. He studied them with considerable curiosity, his eyebrows peaking in a mimic of his father's expression. "Whatcha do with your tail?"

She sighed. "It's a little hard to explain, smallfry."

"Grown-up stuff, huh?"

"You could call it that." She ruffled his dark hair and glanced around the main room of the house. When she'd awakened to a gray but calm morning, there'd been no sign of Drake. That had been a blessing. She'd wanted a chance to talk with the boy, to ask him not to reveal her secret. But she did need information, and maybe a child who wasn't steeped in prejudice against different sorts of people would be the perfect source.

"Matt, honey, do you know anything about mermaids?"

"Sure. I gots a videotape of *The Little Mermaid.*"

"What's a videotape?"

He looked at her as if even the most ignorant of humans would know the answer to that question. "It's what you put in the VCR and watch when there's nothin' on the TV satellite dish."

"Oh. Then it's not about a real mermaid?"

"Uh-uh. Lillian got it for me. It's a kinda sissy story about a girl."

Aria was definitely having trouble keeping up with the youngster. "Who's Lillian?"

"She keeps house for Dad and cleans the cabins when people stay there. Stuff like that. And when Dad goes on a charter, Lil watches out for me. But we don't call it baby-sitting 'cause I'm not a baby anymore."

Aria nodded, though she didn't entirely understand all the nuances of Matt's comments. "What about other mermaids? *Real* ones? Have you heard any stories?"

"I dunno. I heard they gots one at Sechelt, but I never seen it."

Her hopes soared. "Are you sure? There's a mermaid at this place called Sechelt?" Where there was one, there could be more, even an entire village.

He lifted his shoulders in a shrug.

"Do you think your father would take me there?"

"I guess. If you asked him."

Oh, she would. As soon as possible.

Masculine footsteps approaching on the dock suggested Drake was about to reappear.

Aria knelt in front of Matt. She framed his face—an adorable, dark-eyed replica of his father's—between her hands. "Remember, my being a mermaid is *our* secret. Right?"

"Sure. But I don't think Dad would be m-mad or anything."

She hugged the boy. Risking a human male's fury—particularly one who was strangely appealing—was something she wanted to avoid. "Then he won't mind if we have this little secret between us, will he?"

DRAKE OPENED the front door and immediately sensed there was a conspiracy afoot. Meanwhile, Buffy, who'd been trailing him around the dock, squeezed past him through the open door and raced directly for Aria.

"Hi, guys," Drake said, playing it casual.

Aria and Matt jumped apart as if they'd been shot by a couple of harpoons.

"Hey, Dad, did you know—"

Aria clamped a hand on the boy's shoulder. "Did the storm do much damage?" she asked.

"Not really." His gaze collided with sea green eyes, and his body reacted instinctively, hard and fast. Gritting his teeth, he shrugged out of his rain gear and draped it on a clothes rack by the door. "You two have breakfast yet?"

"I can fix Aria some cereal," Matt volunteered.

"That's good, son. You do that." Purring loudly, Buffy rubbed against Aria's legs. "And take your cat with you, Matt. She's been acting weird all morning."

Scooping up the cat under one arm, the boy went into the kitchen.

"So how are you feeling this morning?" Drake asked as he strolled into the room. She looked terrific. In spite of the bandage on her forehead, her color was good. She wasn't wearing a trace of makeup, yet her skin glowed with beauty and good health. Her lips were naturally rosy, their fullness perfectly designed for a man to kiss. Those dynamite sea green eyes met his gaze frankly, framed by silver-blond lashes. He'd never thought anyone would look quite so good wearing his old shirt.

"I'm quite well, thank you."

"Then after breakfast I'll take you to... Where do you want to go?"

"To Sechelt?" There was more question than statement in her response.

"You're from the mainland?"

"Not exactly. I thought I might be able to find some friends there."

Another evasive response, Drake thought. "Look, Aria, if you're in trouble maybe I can help."

"I don't think so. But if you'd take me..."

His eyes narrowed. He really hated secrets and women who kept them. "I've gotta take Matt into the village to get him a new jacket. Then, if the weather holds, we'll motor over to Sechelt." Assuming the police didn't want to ask Aria a few questions themselves.

"Come on, let's eat," he told her.

When he entered the kitchen, he discovered Lillian Assu had already arrived via the back door to the houseboat and was helping Matt get the cereal down from the cupboard.

"Good morning, boss man," she said cheerily. She was broad-faced and broad-hipped, her black hair laced with gray. In Drake's view, every year Lillian aged simply added more fodder to her catalog of information about the residents of Oyster Island. "That was some blow we had, wasn't it? We got enough driftwood up on our beach to last—" She spotted Aria and her mouth stopped flapping.

Drake cringed. He wasn't eager to explain a woman in his house, or the fact that he'd slept on the couch last night. "Lillian, this is Aria. The storm kind of—"

"Land's sake, honey. Is that the best this man could do for clothes for you?" Lillian barked a laugh. "He sure ain't no French fashion designer, is he?"

"It was very generous of Drake to loan me—"

"I don't exactly have a lot of women's clothes stashed around here," he said defensively.

"And whose fault is that?" Lillian challenged. "Could have most any woman on the island, if you had a mind to."

"Which I don't." He grabbed for the carton of milk before Matt's elbow knocked it over.

"Haven't seen you around the island before," Lillian continued, looking toward Aria. "You must be new."

"Yes, quite new," Aria agreed.

"She's just visiting. After breakfast I'm going to take her into the village—"

"Dressed like that? What a hoot! Honey, take some advice from ol' Lil. You show up in town in that getup, and you'll be beatin' off the menfolk with a stick. And you better be sure you got a big 'un, too."

Aria eyes widened. "It's all I have to wear."

"You're scaring her, Lillian. Ease up."

"She used to have a t-tail," Matt said.

Drake shot him a curious look. He was going to have to limit how much TV the boy could watch. His imagination was going crazy. "Eat your cereal, son."

"What in tarnation happened to your clothes, honey?"

"She lost 'em in the storm, okay? You're butting into things that are none of your business, Lil." Not that Drake could explain the situation very well himself.

Silenced for the moment, the housekeeper eyed Aria speculatively. "Seems to me my niece is about your size. I could run home and pick up a few things, if you'd like."

"I don't want to be a bother." The cat threaded her way between Aria's legs, and she nudged Buffy away.

"It's no bother, honey. Telling all my old cronies about finding you here, dressed like that, will be worth any trouble that comes my way. I can promise you that."

Looking a little nonplussed, Aria said, "That's very kind of you."

Drake glowered at Lillian. "Could you just go do it, Lil? Now?" The unrepentant gossip was right, Drake belatedly realized. He couldn't very well take Aria into town wearing his old shirt and a pair of his sweat socks. Hell, you couldn't even tell she had his shorts on. She looked sexy and downright indecent. Dudley, at the general store, would have a field day at Aria's expense. And it didn't bear thinking that Chuck Lampert might be hanging around there, too. His childhood friend and best buddy would razz him unmercifully, given half the chance. There'd be no end to it.

"Whatever you say, boss man." Lillian gave him a sly wink. "I'll be back before you can even miss me."

"I'll miss you like a toothache," he countered gruffly. But the fact was, he loved the nosy old busybody. She'd insinuated herself into his life when he'd been a smart-mouth kid and, in spite of his best efforts to avoid it, she'd been like a mother to him. There'd been a lot of days over the past twenty years that he didn't know what he would have done without Lil. But no way was he gonna tell her that. She'd simply give him more grief about needing a wife to take care of him.

"Come on, you two," he said after Lillian left. "Let's get breakfast over with."

ARIA CONCLUDED that eating cereal was a little like grazing on dried seaweed. She sighed. She'd give her left tail fin for a little fresh oyster meat. Crab would be nice, too. But, of course, she didn't have any fins to spare at the moment.

Which was just as well, since with fins she never would have been able to pull these tight-fitting trousers up over her hips. Lillian had called them jeans.

"Mind you, my niece is only twelve, my sister's youngest," Lillian explained. They were in the bedroom trying on several sets of clothes she'd brought from her home. "The fit may be a bit snug. But then, you're not much bigger than her."

Aria gave one last tug.

"Perfect," Lillian announced. "That oughta catch Drake's eye in a hurry."

"I'm not sure I want to catch his eye." Or any other human male's.

"Why not? He's a fine man. Hardworking. Honest. Got a little money put by, I imagine. A girl could do worse, I'll tell you."

Aria's natural curiosity prodded her. "You've known Drake a long time?"

"His mama—bless her heart—and me were good friends. When she passed on, Drake was only a skinny, scared ten-year-old. I sort of took him under my wing. Not that he thought I needed to."

"Why is it Drake has no female companion?"

"A wife, you mean? Heck, he had one—Matt's mother. She was a firecracker, she was. A little too wild for him, but prettier than a skyrocket. He fell for her—hook, poles and live bait. But they married too young, and she couldn't settle down. Had a roving eye, if you know what I mean. They had Matt—one of those seven-month deals that had everybody countin' on their fingers—and then somethin' went bad wrong." Lillian shook out a sweater and handed it to Aria. "I figured it would work out, but the next thing I knew, Janie's run off and left Drake with the boy. Like to have broke his heart, I'll tell you that."

"There's been no other woman since?" Aria pulled the sweater over her head.

"Nope. The man's dead set against it. 'Course, all it might take is the right woman to come along to change his mind." She eyed the unmade bed. "You interested in giving it a try?"

"No, I don't plan to be here long." Aria doubted Drake would think a mermaid was a suitable partner, particularly once she got her tail back.

"Pity. He could use a little lovin'. He's been alone too long."

"He has Matt. He seems very fond of the boy."

Lillian placed a pair of shoes on the floor and Aria wiggled her feet into them. They pinched. She decided she preferred to wear just socks, but supposed that wasn't acceptable for humans.

"Oh, he's a good papa, Drake is, and Matt's as sweet as a button. But a man needs more than that.

A man needs a woman and for more than the obvious reason. Not that they always understand the difference themselves." She barked a deep-throated laugh. "Fact is, sometimes it takes a sledgehammer to make 'em see the light."

"Wouldn't that hurt?"

Lillian sputtered another laugh. "Oh, honey, you are a piece of work. I do believe if you was interested, you'd spruce up Drake's life just fine."

Aria supposed she ought to be pleased with Lillian's vote of confidence. But she still felt slightly intimidated around Drake, in spite of the tingling sensation she got whenever he looked at her. Or maybe because of it.

It would be much better if she could find a colony of merpeople and never have to deal with the problems of becoming a human permanently. Or the process necessary to go about it.

She glanced at the cat, who had made herself at home curled up on the bed. The feline gazed at her with big yellow eyes. *Decidedly hungry eyes.*

Yes, finding her own people was a much better choice.

When she walked out of the room, she met Drake in the hallway. He gaped at her with eyes fully as hungry as the cat's, but far more dark and intriguing.

"I guess I'm ready to go now," she said.

His gaze swept over her in a slow perusal that raised her temperature by several degrees. "Lil's right. Except I'm gonna find the stick and it's going to be the biggest log I can lift."

He turned and walked away, leaving Aria feeling as though she'd been caught in a heated whirlpool and then dragged down into a maelstrom, where she'd never be able to draw a steady breath again.

THEY GLIDED through the water as fast as a killer whale and just as smoothly; a wake veed from the bow, rippling the dark, tranquil waters of the strait. Overhead, a pair of gulls cawed in greeting to a friend perched on a rock at the edge of a thickly forested shoreline. The clouds hung low and threatening.

Wide-eyed, Aria clung to the railing of Drake's boat. Air damp with the continuing threat of rain tugged at the ends of her hair. The speeding sensation of moving over water so swiftly was exhilarating, and she smiled in spite of her concerns for the future. Of course, she'd once ridden in a dingy that had broken loose from a larger boat, and her stepmother had been known to pirate a small motor launch to help her lure a sailor from his ship, but, to a mermaid, the speed of Drake's boat was extraordinary.

"I always wondered what it would be like to be a sailfish," she shouted over the noise of the engine. "The view from up here is incredible."

"What?" Drake called back from his place at the wheel, the wind whipping his dark hair across his forehead in a fascinating sweep. Matt was standing in front of him on a small box, steering as if he was the captain of the ship instead of his father. "We can't hear you."

She waved to them but elected not to repeat her comment. Drake might think it quite odd that she'd never been on a boat before.

Drake returned her wave, thinking he'd never seen anyone so excited about a boat ride. Her smile was absolutely radiant, in brilliant contrast to the overcast day. The sweater Lillian had provided, so soft-looking his fingers ached to touch it, molded against her body, outlining every delectable curve and swell. She had to be freezing, but you'd never know it. She stood facing into the wind, her hair blowing, the color on her cheeks rosy with the chill in the air.

Damn, how he wanted to take her into his arms at that moment.

Unfortunately, he didn't see any way he could leave the helm under the sole guidance of a six-year-old boy.

Likely Aria wouldn't be all that pleased with the prospect, either.

How, he wondered, could a woman who was so evasive about her past and how she had arrived at Hart's Cove have him fantasizing about romantic gestures, when she hadn't exactly come on to him? Hadn't at all, he corrected. From his perspective, she'd been the epitome of discretion.

Except she hadn't been in the least modest about her sexy, *naked* body.

Damn! Clearly he didn't understand squat about women.

He slowed the engine as he entered the bay. Nearly a dozen fishing boats were tied up at the dock, and two float planes, Chuck Lampert's and a transient plane had been wheeled up onto the sandy beach. Not exactly a metropolitan harbor, but Drake liked it just fine.

AS THE BOAT PULLED into the harbor at Oyster Bay, panic twisted through Aria's midsection. This was a *town*. Several wooden buildings formed a string of dirty pearls just opposite the dock. *Six* buildings, to be exact. The village Drake had spoken about was *huge*.

Though Aria was aware of much larger cities, she'd never been this close to even a small one. And there were people there, too. Strangers.

Panic stroked a finger down her spine. How should she act? By all the sea gods, she hoped she wouldn't fall over her own two feet!

Slowing, Drake nudged the boat against the dock. "Get the bowline, Aria, and tie it off for us."

"Right." He wanted her to leap over the side of the boat, land on the dock with a rope in her hands and then make a sailor's knot? Clearly he didn't know what he was asking of a person who only yesterday had been the proud owner of a beautiful silver tail, and who only understood his sailor jargon because she was particularly adept at eavesdropping on passing sailors.

She took a deep breath and did as she'd been told, grateful she hadn't fallen either on the dock or into the harbor waters.

After this stop in the village, they'd go on to Sechelt. There she would be able to locate other merpeople, and that would be the end of her stay with humans.

Slanting Drake a glance as he moved about the boat deck, she wondered why that thought made her feel as though she'd be missing some very crucial element in her life.

A few minutes later, Drake finished securing the boat to the mooring, tugging the knots more tightly than Aria had managed in her efforts at the unfamiliar task.

As they started to walk toward the shore, Aria reached out for Matt. "Take my hand, small-fry."

The boy looked up at her as if she'd committed some heinous crime. "I'm not gonna get lost or nuthin'. I've been here a zillion times."

"Well, I haven't, Matt. I could use your help." In spite of the cool air, sweat beaded her forehead. She fought the fear of the unknown that threatened to drive her back into the sea, legs or not.

After a moment of hesitation, he slipped his small hand into hers and solemnly vowed, "It's okay, Aria. I'll take care of you."

Chapter Three

Drake pulled open the door of the general store. He pretty well expected raised eyebrows from whomever might be loitering around the potbellied stove. Catcalls wouldn't have surprised him, either.

He was right.

The storekeeper and Chuck Lampert greeted Aria's arrival with wide-eyed, dropped-jaw, drooling masculine appreciation. Only the whistles were missing, mostly because the two of them couldn't get their mouths closed.

Drake slid his hand to the small of Aria's back in a blatant display of possessiveness. Damned if he'd give Lampert and Dudley an inch when it came to Aria. If he did, they'd take a mile. Particularly Lampert, who was bound to ride him hard just for showing up in town with a gorgeous woman in tow.

Giving your best buddy a hard time was practically a full-time hobby in Oyster Bay.

He set his jaw. This wasn't going to be easy.

"Morning, Dudley," Drake said. "My boy's

arms are shooting out of his jacket. You got something warm that will last him the winter?''

''Along the back wall. Have a look.'' The store's proprietor, with a prematurely receding hairline at the front and a wispy blond fringe ten inches long at the back, waved him toward the back of the store. His lecherous smile was strictly intended for Aria.

''Yo, Drake!'' Lampert drawled with a cocky grin. He was sitting with his chair tilted back, balancing it on two legs, and his arms were crossed in an arrogant pose. ''Haven't you got a 'hello' for your ol' buddy?''

''Hated to wake you up. From the looks of you, I thought you must have had a hard night.''

''No such luck,'' he said with a laugh, eyeing Aria as he responded. ''How 'bout you?''

''Not your business, Lampert.'' Drake didn't figure it was his buddy's concern that he'd scooped a naked woman up out of the drink and then had spent the night tossing and turning on the couch while she'd been asleep in his bed. That wouldn't do his macho image much good, and he and Chuck had a friendly rivalry going on when it came to women—sort of their own personal liars' club.

Not that Chuck wasn't fully aware Drake had no interest in a long-term relationship with a woman. He'd sworn off getting serious with women five years ago, after Janie walked out on him. But maybe even Chuck wasn't entirely aware of how deep the wound had cut—or how it still festered deep in his gut.

Part of the game they played was not to reveal too much. Drake figured that was a guy thing.

"So, did you bring your lady friend in to admire my prizewinning catch?" He thumbed over his shoulder, gesturing toward the stuffed white sea bass mounted on the wall above him. Nearly four feet long, it was a classic catch, one the entire village was still talking about. Hell, everybody along the Sunshine Coast of B.C. knew about it. All part of their game of one-upmanship, Lampert never missed a chance to bring up the subject. Or rub it in.

But this was a sensitive subject. The guy with the biggest fish mounted at Dudley's store was top dog when it came to charter-fishing guides. Drake didn't like being second best, not even to his buddy. "You know that fish was mine," he muttered.

"Hey, man, your line broke. You never should have chased after this baby into the narrows on a tidal exchange." Chuck's innocent shrug was too smug. "Besides, can I help it if the fish liked my bait better than yours?"

"Like hell. You ran across my line, Lampert. On purpose."

Chuck responded with a shake of his head that denied Drake's accusation. "Hey, I saved you from your reckless ways just like the time I hauled you out of the gym before Big Blotto could catch you peeking into the girls' dressing room."

Unable to keep a straight face, Drake released a strangled laugh. "That poor principal was pathetic, wasn't he? But remember, I was lookin' through the hole *you* drilled.''

A delicate, feminine hand wrapped itself around Drake's biceps. Drake shot Chuck a smug grin that topped his buddy's for overacting.

"Yes, sweetheart," he said pointedly and plenty loud enough for Chuck to hear—and to know to keep his distance. "What can I do for you?"

"Matt is waiting for you," she said, her eyes filled with surprise. Her lyrical voice burrowed under Drake's skin, almost making him forget that he was putting on a show for his old friend.

"Yeah, right." He swallowed hard. "I'm coming."

As Drake turned and ushered her down an aisle toward the back of the store, Aria's gaze hurdled from one unfamiliar item to another, puzzling out their uses. Fascinating as the bits of metal and pottery were, Drake's attitude toward the other man in the store was even more intriguing. He seemed to be laying claim to her like a wily shark protects his prey from competing predators. His use of an endearment had certainly startled her.

And pleased her, too, she thought with a secret, feminine smile.

"That sea bass was not so large," she said, feeling a surge of loyalty that made her want to encourage the man who had rescued her from the storm. She had the strangest desire to palm his whiskered jaw, to feather a straying lock of his dark hair back from his forehead.

"Bigger than any I've caught, or at least landed," he grumbled with an unconcerned shrug.

"I could help you find even bigger fish."

He shot her a skeptical look. "Oh? You've caught fish bigger than that monster bass?"

"Not exactly," she hedged. The fish mounted on the wall was nearly as large as many mermaids, and its tail was much the same shape, hardly the delicate morsel she preferred. Any bigger, and the bass would have been able to make *her* his meal. She shuddered at the possibility.

"But you're an expert at fishing?"

"I know how to find fish, if that's what you're asking." A mermaid was particularly adept at detecting movement under the water, which included fish swimming within a half mile or so. It was part of a merperson's survival skills. After all, she wouldn't want to be surprised by the arrival of a killer whale or a shark bent on a feeding frenzy.

"Just where is it you've done all this trophy fishing?"

"All over the world," she answered vaguely, though amid tropical islands would have been a more accurate reply.

"Great. I'll take you along on my next charter and tell the guys I've got an unbeatable fish detector on board."

"If you'd like," she agreed with an easy smile, before remembering she'd be leaving Drake soon. An ache rose in her chest, and she forcefully set the feeling aside. It would be much better if she could return to her own people rather than risk the danger of lingering among humans.

"Look, Dad, I found a j-j-jacket for Aria." The boy held up a black coat as shiny as the skin of a seal, the collar trimmed with silver that glistened under the overhead lights.

In spite of herself, Aria sighed, "Oh, it's beautiful. But I really don't need—"

"That sweater you're wearing isn't nearly warm enough for this weather," Drake said. "Here, try it on."

"Really, I can't—"

Refusing to take no for an answer, he helped her on with the jacket. The lining was a soft fur that caressed her with the promise of warmth on the coldest day. As he lifted her hair to clear the collar, a heated shiver sped down her spine, and she had a deep sense that his ability to keep her warm against the worst arctic chill would be even greater than the heaviest coat. He toyed with the thickness of her hair, threading his fingers through the weight. His breath was as soft as a summer breeze across her cheek. Achingly sweet.

As though unaccustomed to remaining upright, her legs seemed to lose their strength, and she leaned into him. His chest was so broad, his arms so strong, he held her easily. For a brief span of time, she felt their hearts beating in a slow, heavy rhythm that echoed the pulse low in her body.

He cleared his throat, abruptly took her shoulders and set her upright again. "It seems to fit okay."

"You look real p-pretty in it, Aria." The boy sent an adoring smile her way.

Aria regained her balance, though her head still spun with the feel of Drake's body so close to hers. "Thank you, Matt, but your father doesn't have to—"

"Yeah, I do." Stepping away from her, Drake yanked a child's jacket from the rack. "Try this one, son."

"Da-ad! That one's p-pink! It's for a *g-girl*," Matt wailed.

Drake stared at the garment incredulously. "You're right. Brown would be better." What the hell had he been thinking about?

The liquid flow of Aria's hair through his fingers.

Her fragrance that was as tantalizing as the sea on a summer day.

The soft molding of her body against his.

Turning, he pulled the first jacket his hand touched from the boy's rack. "This one look better?"

Matt rolled his eyes. "I'm not a b-baby, Dad."

Drake supposed his son was right. The coat he'd picked was for a two-year-old. Clearly he wasn't thinking straight. And Aria knew it. Her sea green eyes sparkled with amusement—at his expense. In response, his heart raced, sending a heady sensation reeling through his body.

"Why don't I help you choose one?" she suggested to Matt.

Grateful to be relieved of the responsibility for

making a decision, Drake studied his son and Aria as they poked through the coats. She had an uncanny ability to get close to the boy, hunkering down to his level physically and enjoying the same youthful enthusiasm for a shopping trip. In contrast, Drake had always felt a little awkward handling this part of his parental role.

A few minutes later Matt had made his choice.

"It's a little big, don't you think?" Drake questioned. The bulky down jacket made Matt look like a round, toasted marshmallow.

"I'll g-grow into it, Dad. I'm almost big."

"Yeah, you sure are, little chip." He knelt and pulled his son into his arms. Over the top of the boy's head, his gaze collided with sea green eyes. An overwhelming sense of gratitude, at least he thought that was what it was, spiraled through him. He could see her pulse ticking in her throat, and he wanted to kiss her there along the ivory column of her neck.

And he had no business thinking like that. Trying to fool Chuck into thinking he had something going with Aria was one thing. But actually *doing* anything about it was a whole different story, one he didn't want to contemplate.

Driving the unwanted thoughts from his mind, he said, "Okay, guys, let's get this stuff paid for and then we'll go have some ice cream."

Matt cheered.

"Ice cream?" Aria questioned.

Drake frowned. "You do like ice cream, don't you?"

"I, ah, well, maybe."

He eyed her speculatively. In his experience, there wasn't a woman alive who could resist a dish of double-double chocolate, to-die-for ice cream. Nor was there one who would have forgotten the flavor, no matter how big a bump she'd gotten on her head.

Assuming Aria wasn't putting on an act, she was in a class by herself. Drake had some serious doubts that was the case, at least in terms of her ability to recall her past.

In other arenas, she was certainly one of a kind.

For the moment, however, his goal was to keep Aria and his son occupied while he went in search of the local police. He had some serious questions to ask that Aria didn't appear willing to answer.

Returning to the front counter with the jackets, Drake said, "You wanna ring these up, Dudley?"

"Sure thing." He checked the tag on Matt's coat and punched in the amount on the cash register. "Good lookin' woman you got with you."

"She's just passing through."

"That a fact? Chuck and me was hoping she was planning to hang around. We could use a little somethin' to liven up this place."

Drake's gaze shot to where Aria was examining some canned goods on a shelf. Matt was with her. And Chuck was moving in on them both with that slick, lady-killer smile of his.

An emotion suspiciously like jealousy snaked through Drake's gut.

"Come on, son, we're about ready to go," he called. "Bring Aria."

Dudley rang up the second jacket. "You wanna put this on your bill?"

"Yeah, that'll be fine."

Aria joined him at the counter with two cans in her hand. "Are there really oysters inside these?" she asked Drake.

"That's what the label says."

She looked at them wistfully.

"You like oysters?" he asked.

"They're one of my favorites." Her eyes widened with a silent plea.

Drake resisted that come-hither look with as much success as a sand bar resisted being washed away by a high tide. He took the cans from her. "Put these on the tab too," he told Dudley, placing them on the counter.

His reward was a melt-your-heart smile from Aria.

As she walked away to examine a rack of scenic postcards designed to attract the attention of tourists, Dudley said under his breath, "I guess she thinks you need to get your juices going, huh?"

"What do you mean by that crack?"

"Hey, man, everybody knows oysters are a sure-fire aphrodisiac. Perfect cure for the guy who's having trouble—"

"Knock it off, Dudley!" Heat sped to his cheeks.

Dammit, he hadn't blushed in years. And he sure as hell didn't need his testosterone level raised. His hormones already revved into overdrive any time Aria was around. It was that walk of hers, that damn sexy way she swayed her hips and seemed to glide with every step. Or maybe it was that tumble of blond hair his fingers itched to comb. Or those impish, sea green eyes.

Oh, hell! An aphrodisiac was the last thing he wanted before putting some much-needed distance between himself and the mysterious Aria.

AFTER DEPOSITING Matt and Aria at the only place resembling a restaurant in the village, Drake checked out the small police station at the end of the street. With one officer to patrol several islands, he was lucky to find William Wallace at Oyster Bay.

He was sitting with his feet propped up on his desk, reading a paperback.

"Looks like you've got the island crime wave under control," Drake kidded.

Willy's feet hit the floor with a bang, and he gave Drake an embarrassed grin. "Just like you, my business drops off after the tourists go home. Thank goodness."

"Yeah, but you still get paid."

"How true. What can I do for you?" Like Lillian, Willy was a member of the Kwakiutl Indian tribe and knew the islands as though the landscape had been etched into his ethnic memory. Drake shared a similar ancestry, though somewhat diluted by English settlers.

"I wondered if you had any reports of a missing person. A woman."

"Around here?"

"She could have fallen off a boat in the storm." Or been pushed, he mused.

"I haven't heard anything."

Drake lifted his hip and sat on one corner of the desk. "Could you check it out?"

"Sure. You want to tell me why you're interested?"

"I rescued a woman off the boundary rock at Hart's Cove last night. Says her name's Aria, but she's evasive about how she got there." And he wasn't about to mention she'd been stark naked when he'd found her. That information Drake would keep to himself—and his dreams.

"You thinking foul play? Or some criminal activity?"

"I don't know."

"How old is she?"

Drake wasn't sure. There was an ageless quality to Aria that was also strangely innocent. And very appealing. "Twenty-something, I'd guess. Blonde. Long hair. Green eyes. A little over five feet." His description didn't come close to doing Aria justice—he'd left out the sparkle in her eyes and the way she wrinkled her nose when she smiled. And how her luxurious hair felt in his hands. Those were details he figured Willy could do without.

Scribbling a few notes on a yellow pad, Willy said, "I'll make a couple of calls and let you know if I hear anything."

"Thanks. If the weather holds, I'm taking her over to Sechelt this morning."

"You think that's where she's from?"

"Somehow I don't think so. But that's where she says she wants to go."

ARIA CAST OFF the bowline, relieved to be leaving the village at Oyster Bay. Too many people made her uncomfortable, particularly that Chuck Lampert person at the general store—forget his blond good looks and muscular physique. She supposed he was simply being friendly when he'd sought her out in the store. But the way he looked at her, as if he knew something she didn't, made her uneasy.

His invitation had surprised her, too.

She leaped over the railing and onto the deck as Drake revved the engine, then edged the throttle forward. Her stomach responded to the sudden acceleration with a quick flip-flop. Though she found it exhilarating, she wondered how long it would take to get used to traveling at such high speeds.

And knew with a strangely painful twist in her midsection that if she found a school of merpeople to join, she wouldn't ever learn the answer to that puzzling question.

Standing near Drake as he navigated out of the harbor, she asked, "Have you known Chuck Lampert long?"

"We grew up together."

"Here on the island?"

"Yeah. We've been best buddies since we were about six."

"Oh, I wasn't sure... Then it was all right that he asked me to have sushi with him?"

Drake's attention snapped toward her. "He what?"

"When he learned I enjoy oysters, he thought I might like sushi, too. That's fresh fish cut up—"

"I know what sushi is. What I don't know is why Chuck was asking you—"

"He said he knew of a place on the big island that served particularly good sushi. He offered to fly me there in his float plane. If I was interested."

Drake's expressive eyebrows lowered, and his throat worked convulsively, making Aria wonder if she had said something to upset him.

"So what did you tell my *buddy?*"

"That I was sorry but I wouldn't be here long enough to go with him. Though I've never been in a plane," she sighed wistfully. She'd certainly seen them flying overhead in the clouds, but had never expected to have an opportunity to actually fly in one herself. "It must be even more exciting than riding in a boat."

"Trust me, Aria. Boats are better."

Before she could ask why he thought that, Matt popped up from below deck. "We going to take Aria to Sechelt now?" he asked.

In an affectionate gesture, Drake reached out to

ruffle his son's hair. "That's the plan. We'll tie up at the visitors' dock in the middle of town."

"No, Dad, she doesn't want to go to the t-town. She wants to see the *m-mermaid.*"

Eyebrows peaking, Drake checked over his shoulder to confirm Matt's statement with Aria. The wind feathered a dark lock of hair across his forehead as the boat raced toward the mainland shore. "You want to go to the provincial park?"

"If that's where the mermaid is," she agreed. "Yes, please."

"Why would you want to do that? I don't have any scuba gear on board, and the water is cold enough to freeze the tail off a salmon."

Excitement tightened Aria's chest. Obviously Matt's story of a mermaid was true or Drake would have denied it. The seals and otters who had given her directions along her route north had been right. She simply hadn't traveled far enough in her quest to find another school of merpeople.

"Please," she repeated, hugging her new jacket more snugly around her.

"If that's what you want." With a puzzled shrug, he turned the wheel and set a new course.

Aria faced toward the forested shore, the cold, damp wind bringing tears to her eyes. She'd miss Drake—and his son, of course. They'd both been very kind to her. And Lillian, too. But she was a mermaid and belonged with her own people.

They cruised across the water for some time, Matt proudly steering the boat. Aria remembered how her own father had allowed her to lead the way from one island to another as his band of merpeople migrated. His trust had made her feel proud and very grown-up. Drake was the same kind of caring father.

Filled with nostalgia, she began to hum a song her father had taught her. Soon she was singing a poignant mermaid melody into the wind, and tears were streaming down her face to be whipped away by the chill breeze.

A gloved hand cupped her cheek. She looked up into eyes such a deep brown, they reminded her of the rich, dark chocolate of the ice cream she and Matt had eaten, but far warmer.

"Are you all right?" Drake asked. With his thumb, he wiped away a stray tear.

"I was just thinking about my father."

"Does he live near here."

"No. He died." In a fisherman's net, she thought with a lingering trace of bitterness.

"I'm sorry."

"It wasn't your fault."

His gaze slid over her face, finally settling on her lips. "You sing beautifully. You're very talented."

"Thank you."

He dipped his head toward hers, and Aria was sure he was going to kiss her. Her heart strummed an extra beat. Yes, she'd like, just once, to feel his warm, full lips on hers before she transformed back into a mermaid when she slipped into the water during the next full moon.

"Dad? Are you gonna show Aria the m-mermaid, or what?"

Drake tensed, and his eyes grew shuttered. He backed away.

Taking a deep breath as though she had suddenly forgotten the art of using her lungs, Aria realized they had come to a stop in a small cove. A rugged spit of land protected the sheltered area on the south, and several flat, water-worn rocks rose above the sea, perfect resting places for a weary mermaid.

"This is the place?" she asked.

"It's the home of the Emerald Lady, or so they tell me. I've never seen her myself."

Aria raced to the back of the boat. Climbing over the railing, she squatted on the transom and trailed her hand through the water. Afraid to so much as breathe, she waited for the telltale ripple of fin and tail that would alert her to the slightest sign of life. As the moments passed, her heart sank with disappointment. This was a sterile place, her instincts told her. There was almost no movement through these calm waters and little vegetation. A single perch swam by about thirty yards off shore. Farther out, she sensed a cod feeding on the bottom.

But there were no merpeople here. Not one. She'd have known if there were.

Panic tugged at her hopes like a riptide. "There aren't any mermaids here!" she cried.

Drake's expressive eyebrows dipped. "You can't see her from the surface. She's sixty feet down in the water. It's a bronze statue some guy made, though it's beyond me why he'd go to all that work and then sink her in ten fathoms. He used his wife as a model for the top half of the statue and used a salmon for the tail. Scuba divers make a big deal about checking her out.''

His stunning revelation hit Aria like a blow to her midsection. "The mermaid's not real?"

"She must weigh a ton or more. That's real enough.''

"No, I mean—'' How could she explain to Drake she was looking for something made of flesh and bone, not bronze? "Are there other mermaids? I'd heard—''

"There's supposed to be one in Vancouver Harbor. She's sitting on a rock, or something. It's a statue like the one in Oslo, Norway." His scowl drew a little deeper and tighter. "What's with you and Matt and all this talk about mermaids? Is there some sort of screwy TV contest going on I don't know about?''

Hopes plummeting, Aria sank into a chair at the stern of the boat. An arctic blast swirled around the boat and sent a shiver down her spine. She was lost. There weren't any mermaids in these waters. The otters and seals who had guided her in this direction had been misled by stories of a lifeless statue. If she was to have any chance of surviving the winter, her choices had been narrowed to one.

This was nothing like a contest. For her, finding a school of merpeople had been a matter of life and death. The next best option, with winter approaching, was for her to become pregnant with the milt of a human male—but then she would become permanently human.

She glanced up at Drake. He was indeed handsome in a rather dangerous way. He exuded a sense of self-sufficiency that was intimidating and a little frightening—rather like a killer shark who circled his prey in the full knowledge the quarry was his for the taking. All in all, for a human male, Drake was quite appealing.

Like the stroke of a finger down her spine, a new awareness shuddered through Aria. She was attracted to Drake, and that might make their mating tolerable. Though she hadn't the vaguest idea how to go about the process, she suspected getting close—*very* close—to Drake would be required. Surely such a virile male would have the detailed knowledge necessary to make the consummation successful.

But based on the curious way he was studying her, Aria concluded she should not reveal the decision she'd just made. She wasn't entirely sure he'd be willing to share his milt with her simply to enable her to keep her human form.

Resigned to her fate and determined to get things rolling as soon as possible, she lifted her chin and said, "I'm ready to go now."

"Go where?" he asked.

She stood and moved toward him until their bodies gently collided—his long and strong and excruciatingly potent; hers soft and vulnerable. His eyes widened at the contact as she wrapped her arms around his waist.

"I'm going home with you," she whispered.

Chapter Four

Every muscle in Drake's body went as taut as the lines on a sailboat buffeted by heavy winds. He nearly keeled over, and might have if Aria's arms hadn't been wrapped around his middle. *Intimately* wrapped around his middle.

"Home?" His voice caught, and he cleared his throat.

"The truth is, there's nowhere else I can go."

"You must have friends. Family. Isn't there someone?"

A glint of determination sparked in her sea green eyes, igniting a fire in his belly. "No one."

His arms felt disconnected from the rest of his body as they instinctively slid around her slender figure in response to her embrace. Sweat beaded his forehead. "You, uh, can't stay with us. There's no room."

Ignoring what was going on behind him as he stared at the shoreline, Matt piped up, "She c-could sleep in my room, Dad."

That would be in dangerously close proximity if

Drake were to have any hope of keeping his hands off her. "I don't think that's a good idea, son."

"Why not?" the boy complained. He threw a bit of cracker toward a gull paddling in the water near the rocks. "I gots bunk beds."

"Would it be so awful to have me living with you for a short time? I promise not to cause any trouble," Aria assured him.

She'd be trouble, all right, spelled with a capital *T*. Which also stood for *Temptation*. Drake didn't need that. "Maybe I can hook you up with the Red Cross or somebody who can help you find your family."

"It would be of no use." She shifted her position sightly. Seductively. "I could help you find the fish you search for."

Drake clenched his teeth as need whipped through him. Thank goodness Matt was far more interested in gulls than in his old man. "The charter season is pretty slow right now."

"Come on, Dad. Are we going to stay here all d-day or what?"

Or what sounded like the most likely possibility if Drake didn't put some distance between himself and Aria in a hurry.

Steeling his resolve, he grasped her shoulders and stepped back to arm's length. The gesture didn't do much to cool down his amorous thoughts. "Maybe you can stay with Lillian till we can figure out something else."

Her delectable lips slid into a troubled moue and

she sighed a heart-wrenching sound. "Do you find me so unappealing?" she asked so softly only he could hear her question.

"No, it's not that. It's—" Having her stay with Lillian would provide a little time and distance that would at least allow him to survive without making a fool of himself, until he could figure out where Aria had come from and where she belonged. He hoped. Willy Wallace had damned well better act fast. "You'd be better off with Lil." And so would he.

"I could come visit you at Lil's," Matt said, turning around. "She lets me sometimes."

Aria beamed a smile in the boy's direction, one that made Drake wish he'd been the recipient of her obvious affection. "I'd like that, small-fry."

The boat lifted on a swell and a few raindrops spattered onto the darkly mirrored water. Glancing toward the shore, Drake noted the mist had lowered to hide the trectops, the moisture in the air muffling the sound of wavelets as they lapped against the rocks. The picnic tables situated in shady spots looked damp and uninviting in the chilly gloom.

Toward the straits, the sky looked even more ominous than it did overhead.

"We'd better get going," he said. Deliberately he turned to concentrate on the task of starting the boat and navigating back toward Hart's Cove. It wouldn't do to get lost among these small islands with a new line of storm clouds bearing down on them.

As soon as they cleared the sheltered cove, the

chilling wind and icy rain drove Aria below deck. Disappointment weighed heavily on her spirits. There were no mermaids here, and she had failed dismally in her effort to interest Drake in sharing his milt with her. His reaction had shaken her ego. Among her own people she had been considered quite attractive. Legs, apparently, had detracted from her appeal.

Perhaps she had done something wrong, she thought, though the feel of Drake's strong body brushing against hers had been quite pleasant from her perspective. Evidently he had not felt the same intriguing sensations.

With an irritated sigh, she sat down beside Matt at the half-circle table in the galley. He'd spread out a phalanx of toy characters on the tabletop and was arranging them in neat rows. Unconsciously she smoothed the boy's damp hair away from his face.

Obviously she would have to rely on Lillian's help and advice if she was to achieve her goal. Surely such a kind woman would be able to suggest how Aria might convince Drake to mate with her. It would only take a time or two, she assured herself, hardly a significant inconvenience for a male as virile as Drake.

That he was so resistant to her advances brought a frown to her forehead. Every merman she'd met had been far more eager than Drake, though she had never encouraged a single one.

Drake Hart would simply have to learn that when she made up her mind, she was no fragile minnow to be frightened away by the simple back-pedaling flick of his flipper.

LILLIAN PULLED a sheet from the dryer, billowed it with a quick snap of her wrists, caught the opposite side and began folding it, all in one fluid motion.

"But you can't leave," Drake complained. "Not now."

"My daughter's been ordered to bed till the baby comes. She and her other four youngsters need me, especially with her husband working such long hours at the mill. You'll manage."

"But what about Matt? I've got a charter scheduled next week if the weather clears—"

"Aria can watch the boy, can't she? And if she needs a break, you can always take Matt over to Tommy Kelly's house. They play just fine together. His mother would watch out for Matt for a few hours if you get in a pinch." She straightened the corners of the sheet and tugged them smooth. "And there's nothing hard about cleaning around the house and making a few meals. Aria will do fine."

Aria probably would, but Drake was less sure of himself. They'd returned from Sechelt only to discover Lillian in a frenzy of activity, getting last-minute details taken care of so she could leave for her daughter's home at the far end of the island.

"If your daughter needs that much help, maybe Aria ought to go with you," he suggested in a desperate effort to avoid being left on his own to face temptation.

Hugging the folded sheet to her ample bosom, Lillian eyed him speculatively. "Now why would you be so all-fired anxious to get rid of Aria?"

"I'm not. It's just that—"

"A pretty little thing like her scares the bejeebers out of you?"

He gave her his most ferocious scowl, which she totally ignored.

"Seems to me it'd be a real treat for you and Matt to have a woman around the house again. Somebody a lot younger 'n prettier than me. She's not going to bite, you know."

"I know," he grumbled.

"And Matt does need some lookin' after, even if he doesn't think so. You can't keep an eye on him a hundred percent of the day."

Drake jammed his hands in his pockets. Lil was right, dammit! Matt needed someone around, when he couldn't be there. He considered sending Aria away and hiring a girl from the village. But with the part-timers who helped during tourist season gone from the island, and school in session, he'd be unlikely to find anyone available.

Placing the folded sheet on top of the dryer, Lillian yanked out another one and repeated the process. "I'll show Aria what needs doing before I leave. With business this slow, she'll catch on fast enough."

Defeated, Drake asked, "How long do you think you'll be gone?"

"The baby's not due for another two months.

They want her to postpone having him as long as she can.''

He groaned. ''Two months?'' He'd never be able to hold off that long without...well, without getting ''closer'' to Aria—not if she was willing. And from the way she'd acted on the boat that afternoon, he didn't think she'd take much convincing.

Clamping his jaw down tight, he vanquished the heated images that came to mind at the thought of Aria in his arms. If he wanted to avoid being trapped once again by a woman, he would simply have to redouble his efforts to resist falling for her allure. A man could do that.

He didn't necessarily have to like it.

ARIA LIFTED the fist-size rock Matt had brought her and slammed it into the container of oysters. She hardly made a dent in the shiny surface.

How in the name of Neptune was she supposed to make supper for Drake and his son if she couldn't even get to the oysters? She'd seen otters open clams this way a thousand times. Why wouldn't it work for her?

With a quick flick of her head, she flipped her hair back behind her shoulder and tried the rock again with the same dismal result. Her hand stung.

''What the devil are you doing?''

Aria whirled at the sound of Drake's voice. ''I'm fixing supper. Lillian said I should.'' The house-keeper had offered a whole raft of other instructions, too, none of which included how to open this container. Or get Drake to mate with her. Lil had been in such a rush, there hadn't been time to ask the necessary questions.

Drake's dark-eyed gaze shot to the container and back to Aria. "Oysters?"

"They're very tasty."

"That may very well be, but did you think you had to beat them to death first?" His lips twitched into the slightest suggestion of a smile. "Inside the can?"

Her heart struck a heavy beat as though it were trying to escape from her chest. He did have the most inviting mouth, his lips full and sensual. "Well, no..."

"Maybe you ought to consider using a can opener."

"Can opener?" she echoed. What in the world was that?

"Here. Let me." Their fingers brushed as he took the container, and a current of heat swept up her arm. For an instant their eyes locked, and then he stepped away.

Struggling to regain the breath his gaze had stolen from her lungs, Aria watched in quiet admiration as he used a purring device to lift the lid from the can. The fabric of his heavy shirt strained across his shoulders, suggesting a well-muscled physique. She thought if he were a merman, Drake would be a powerful swimmer, and every mermaid would be vying to swim beside him. It stung her pride that he had so little interest in her.

Setting the lid aside, he drained the excess liquid from the can into the sink.

"You think you can handle opening the other can?" he asked.

She leaped at the opportunity to get closer to him, even in the guise of using the strange device. "If you would show me," she suggested innocently.

Eyebrows lowered, he cocked his head to the side and studied her with keen intensity. "Where the hell have you been living that you don't know how to use an electric can opener?"

"It was a very remote area," she hedged.

"No electricity?"

"No."

"But you can't remember specifically where you lived?"

"Not exactly."

"Right." He didn't seem at all satisfied with her response. "There's a hand can opener in the drawer. You could have used that."

"I guess I didn't think of it." Why would she, since she'd never had a need to open a can before? "I usually eat my oysters fresh."

Picking up the second can, Drake studied the label and wondered if there was any truth in Dudley's story about oysters increasing a man's sexual performance. And if so, did they have the same effect on a woman? Not that he intended to put them to the test. "Any particular reason why you're so anxious to fix oysters for dinner?"

"Lillian suggested some other ideas, but I'm not

really all that good at cooking.'' She was much more confident, once shown the intricacies of human mating, she'd be sufficiently skilled at that endeavor.

He lifted a skeptical eyebrow. ''So you come from some remote place, that doesn't have electricity, and you never learned how to cook. You've certainly led a sheltered life, Aria.''

Mentally, Aria began to squirm like a worm caught on a fisherman's hook. She wasn't accustomed to lying. If only he didn't look so dark and foreboding, she might risk telling him the truth. But she had a great deal to lose if she made a wrong decision. Her life hung in the balance.

Before she could compose a response, he said, ''My wife didn't much like to cook, either.''

''I'm sure I can learn if you'll be patient with me.''

''Fortunately I'm not fussy about what I eat.'' He dropped the unopened can back onto the counter. His wife had been a real party animal, more interested in getting a guy hot than in putting a hot meal in his stomach. Drake couldn't help wondering if Aria was the same. ''I think I'll skip the oysters. Hot dogs will do for me and Matt.''

Her eyes widened, and she shot a glance toward Buffy, who'd been curled up in a kitchen chair watching them, ears alert to their conversation. She wondered if the cat was troubled by her owner's preference for eating dogs and decided it was none of her concern. No doubt consuming an assortment of four-legged creatures was some quirk of humans she'd not yet learned about and wasn't in the least interested in pursuing.

"After dinner I'll take you up to the cabins. They're all vacant, so you can have your pick. You'll have more privacy there than you would if you bunked in with Matt."

"Will he be disappointed?" Aria knew she was. Seducing Drake from a distance would make her task doubly difficult.

"He'll get over it. Besides, you'll be around every day until Lil gets back. Matt can be pretty wearing if you're not used to kids. You'll need a break."

"If you say so." Dipping her fingers into the open can of oysters, she tipped her head back and dropped a morsel into her mouth, oddly aware of Drake's dark eyes following her every movement. The familiar flavor was only mildly reassuring and she swallowed with difficulty. If truth be known, she was far more at ease with Matt than his father. But it was Drake whom she needed.

To Aria's great relief, when Drake served dinner, she discovered hot dogs bore no particular resemblance to the four-legged variety; though she doubted the spicy flavor would ever be one of her favorites.

HE'D MADE IT through dinner. That had been a major accomplishment with Aria and Matt engaged in an animated conversation about Power Rangers and assorted other cartoon characters that seemed particularly fascinating to her. He'd felt like the odd man out.

And then he'd shown her to the too-small cabin with the too-narrow beds where she would stay, and he'd felt like a fool. He wanted her in his house, in his bed, and that was the stupidest thing of all. Janie had taught him the consequences of lust. It had been a hell of a painful lesson. He wasn't about to forget that now.

Yanking off his shirt as he prepared for bed, he caught the sound of a woman singing a sultry, seductive melody that plucked at an emotion he had cast aside long ago. He clenched his fists. It was Aria. She was calling to him in a sweet, beguiling voice, and it was either all in his imagination, or a manifestation of his gut-wrenching frustration.

Unable to resist, he shoved the curtain aside and peered through the dark night up toward the cabins situated on the bluff above the cove. He groaned aloud.

Even in the faint light from hidden stars he could see her sitting on a rock, her long, blond hair tumbled in a silver screen around her. She looked so enticing, he ached to go to her. Her song spoke without words of a deep loneliness—his or hers, he couldn't be sure which. The haunting strain lured him. Tempted him. Made him want to climb the highest mountain or dive through the deepest sea to ease the pain that gave power to her song.

Bracing himself on either side of the window, he fought the urge. Sweat sheened his body, and his teeth clenched painfully. He'd learned a hard lesson. One he was determined never to forget.

HE WAS STILL TRYING to concentrate on that lesson a couple of days later when he spotted Aria and Matt together at the end of the dock. He managed to ignore the lyrical sound of her laughter while he repaired one of his bait tanks. As he polished some brass fittings that had turned green in the salt air, he kept one ear cocked, straining to hear their conversation.

Finally, when they became absolutely silent, he gave up his efforts to ignore them and strolled nonchalantly past his boat to where they were both sprawled on the dock, their hands dangling in the water.

Talk about peculiar. The water had to be freezing!

He hunkered down beside them. "What are you two up to?"

"Shh, Dad, Aria's teaching me to catch fish."

"You got a line down there?"

"Uh-uh. She doesn't need one."

Aria smiled up at Drake, a twinkle of mischief in her eyes. "We're getting the fish to come close so we can tickle their tummies."

"You're what?" he sputtered.

"Shh, D-Dad. You gotta be real quiet."

"And patient," Aria added.

"Right." He scowled and peered over the side of the dock. He could just see the shadow of their hands in the dark water, their fingers fluttering.

"There aren't any fish this close to shore, except five-inch shiners."

"Oh, but that's not so." Aria contradicted him in a whisper. "There are several perch nearby, and a school of smelt are swimming just off the point. There will be bass running right behind them."

"There's no way you can know that," he said skeptically. Not unless she had an electronic fish finder down there in the water, and even then she wouldn't necessarily know what kind of fish she'd spotted.

She turned to Matt. "Careful now, small-fry. There's a perch about to nibble on your fingers."

Matt's eyes widened. "I feel him!"

Drake didn't believe a word of it. "Now look, Aria, enough of this crazy—"

"You don't think I can catch a fish with my hand?"

"Nobody can."

Tossing her hair back away from her face, she gave him a smug look. "Watch me."

She made the slightest movement, hardly more than the twist of her wrist, and pulled a ten-inch striped sea perch from the water. It's tail flopped back and forth in a frantic effort to escape.

Drake's jaw dropped. He'd never seen—

"Wow, Aria! You did it! Did you see that, Dad? Did you?"

"I did. But I still don't believe it."

Her thoroughly self-satisfied grin grew broader as

she dropped the fish on the dock at his feet. "Would you like me to catch another for supper?"

Drake resisted the impulse to match her smile with one of his own. "Sure, if you think you can repeat that bit of magic."

"I can even teach you, if you'd like."

Drake had the oddest suspicion she could teach him a whole lot of things.

"I'm gonna catch one this time," Matt insisted. He shoved his hand, which was already red from the cold, back into the water.

"Come on, son, you can't—"

"Let him try. It's not hard, really it isn't."

Drake thought either Aria was crazy, or he was. Probably the latter since he couldn't resist the plea in her voice. "Okay, son, give it a try, then you have to get busy with your schoolwork."

"Matt is in a school?" Aria asked.

"I home teach him. The kids on the island have to take a ferry to the mainland for regular school, so most of them are home taught until about third grade."

"Shh, you guys. Can't you see I'm trying to c-catch a fish?"

Swallowing a chuckle, Drake ruffled his son's hair without taking his eyes off Aria. What he really wanted to do was run his fingers through her curls and feel their weight in his palms. Her smile softened as though she knew exactly what he was thinking and thought that was a fine idea.

Drake figured he'd be smart if he took a dive into the cove and cooled off.

"I feel one," Matt whispered excitedly.

With a slow, sensual look that raised Drake's temperature by another several degrees, Aria dragged her gaze away from him. "I'll help you, small-fry." Her hand slid into the water next to Matt's without a ripple, like silk on satin. "Tickle him gently. That's right." She paused. "Now."

Their hands came up together, both of them clutching another small perch.

Stunned, Drake rocked back on his haunches. "I'll be damned."

Matt started whooping and hollering loud enough to drive every fish within a mile clear to the opposite shore. Aria looked exceptionally pleased with the trick she'd just pulled off.

In spite of himself, Drake found his lips twitching into a smile, those particular muscles feeling rusty and stiff from disuse. He wondered at the magic that made him suddenly feel so good and knew the credit belonged to Aria.

He hugged his son. "Good job, little chip. Looks like I'll have to start hiring you as a fishing guide."

Aria's heart experienced a strange, rather pleasant squeezing sensation as Drake smiled over Matt's head at her. Had she known the way to gain his attention was to catch a fish or two, she would have filled his entire boat with them. In the future she'd make it a point to do just that.

Matt tugged on Drake's shirt sleeve. "D-Dad, I think we oughta *marry* Aria."

Caught off guard by a coughing attack, Drake lost his balance and fell on his butt. "I, ah, think that idea is a bit premature, little chip."

"But we better do it *soon,* Dad. You wouldn't want Chuck to marry her and then catch all the fish, would you?"

That was not a pleasant prospect, Drake agreed. He shot Aria an apologetic look. "That's not exactly why a man and woman get married, son." Though after his experience with Janie, he wasn't sure what a good reason would be.

Aria's impish eyes crinkled at the edges and she giggled. "Oh? It seems a perfectly good reason to me and Matt."

"Yeah, well, not to me." He levered himself upright. What the hell was the matter with his son? Matt had never acted like this around any other woman he'd brought home, not that there had been many. "If you don't mind, son, leave any future proposals to me. I'm not sure you're ready for a leap into matrimony just yet, and I know damn well I'm not. It'd take me six months—maybe a year—getting to know a woman before I ever popped the question again. *If* I ever did. That'd be my advice to you too, kid."

"Six months is a very long time," Aria said so softly he could barely hear her words.

"Aw, gee..." Matt complained.

Drake ruffled Matt's hair. "Come on, let's get these fish cleaned so we can have them for dinner."

AFTER THE FISH had been cleaned, Matt went back to the house to do his schoolwork with the promise that Drake would join him in a few minutes.

Drake washed down the area where they'd been working, shooing Buffy away in the process. That darn cat had certainly been pesky since Aria arrived, almost as intrigued with their houseguest as he was.

"Who is that?" Aria asked, gesturing toward the shore end of the dock.

He glanced the direction she indicated before turning the hose off. "James Wamish. He's the island lighthouse keeper. Been doing it for sixty years, and his father had the job before that."

Aria watched with interest as the man came toward them. His coloring was as dark as Drake's, but his long hair had turned as white as the foam that rode the top of a breaking wave. For a moment she felt a stab of nostalgia for her father. His hair, too, had turned white with age and increasing wisdom.

"Hello, youngster," the old man said, extending his hand to Drake. He eyed Aria speculatively and gave her a toothless grin. "Looks like your clientele is finally getting a little class."

Returning James's smile, Aria felt heat color her cheeks.

"This is Aria," Drake said gruffly. "She's, ah, filling in for Lil. Temporarily."

"Imagine that." James's smile grew a bit wider.

"I'm not so old I can't think of a few ways she could help out around here that Lillian couldn't."

"You want something, James? Or are you just looking to make conversation."

"Well, the fact is...I thought you'd like to know I caught sight of the Salmon Woman last night."

"You what?" Drake barked.

"The Salmon Woman, that's what. You've heard about her."

Curious, Aria said, "I haven't."

"It's an old Indian legend about why the salmon always return to these waters," Drake explained. He rolled up the hose and draped it over a hook. "And if James saw her last night, you can figure he'd been tippling on a bottle of Jim Beam." He glanced again at his friend. "Thought you gave that up, James."

"I did. And I know what I saw."

In a gesture of comradery, Drake looped his arm around the older man's shoulders. "Come on, James. Let's see if a cup of coffee will sober you up."

James grunted a dissenting response. "Prettiest tail I ever did see."

Chapter Five

Aria nearly fell over her own unfamiliar feet in her excitement to keep up with Drake and his friend.

"Where did you see the Salmon Woman?" she asked breathlessly. Their long strides gobbled up the dock in big chunks compared to her shorter, more tentative steps.

"Don't listen to anything this old man says," Drake said over his shoulder. "When he's been nipping at the bottle, he's half-blind and a hundred percent crazy."

"That's not so," James grumbled, although he elbowed Drake's ribs good-naturedly, one friend to another.

Aria gritted her teeth. She *wanted* to hear what James had to say. There might be a whole school of salmon people who migrated through these waters. If that was so, surely they would accept her into their community, or know with some confidence where she might find her own merpeople.

Determined to get some answers, she followed them into the kitchen. Matt was sitting at the table, a book open in front of him as he laboriously made curious marks on a separate sheet of paper. The boy jumped up from his chair.

"Hi, Papa James. Did you see the fish me an' Aria caught? She taught me to tickle their tummies."

The older man laughed a deep, robust sound as he hugged the boy. "Sounds to me like you're as fine a fisherman as your old man."

"G-gonna be even b-better."

Smiling at their affectionate exchange, Aria said, "Shall I fix coffee, Drake? Lillian showed me how." Though the instructions had been hurried, Aria was sure she remembered them.

"Sure." He shrugged out of his jacket and hung it on an already-crowded coatrack by the door.

Examining the pot, Aria decided she'd try a little coffee herself. That meant there'd be three people drinking coffee, she reasoned, so she estimated how much water would be needed and filled the pot to that point. From the cupboard she took down a tin of coffee. Lillian had assured her that the premeasured packages made perfect coffee every time.

She emptied three of them—one packet of dry coffee for each cup—into the nesting place above the pot, poured the appropriate amount of water into the reservoir and flicked on the switch. Smiling smugly at how cleverly she'd remembered Lillian's instructions, she turned back to the men sitting at the table.

Before she could even begin questioning James

about the Salmon Woman, there was a knock on the door.

Drake let in a man who was tall and lanky with a shock of curly red hair. The new arrival added his jacket to the rack by the door.

"Aria, this is Joe Voulgan," Drake said, wondering why Joe had shown up at his house. He couldn't remember the guy ever dropping by to visit before. They'd been in school at the same time, but Joe was several years younger than Drake, and they hadn't been close friends. "He and his folks own an oyster lease up island."

"Oyster lease?" she asked.

"They raise 'em commercially."

She nodded.

Smiling like an awestruck adolescent, Joe offered her a plastic bag heavy with oysters. "They said in the village you particularly like oysters. I thought you might like some fresh ones. I eat a lot of 'em myself."

"How nice of you." Aria's smile was enough to light up the entire kitchen as she took Joe's offering.

Hell, it was bright enough to light up the entire Sunshine Coast on a cloudy day, and Drake knew that was exactly why Joe had shown up. News of Aria's presence was spreading pretty damn fast around the island, along with her taste for oysters.

"We were just going to have some coffee. Sit down if you want some," he all but ordered Joe, who complied too easily for his liking, a sappy grin on the guy's face, his eyes glued to Aria's every movement. His tongue was practically dragging on the floor.

Delighted with the gift, Aria placed the bag on the counter. What a thoughtful young man! But if he wanted coffee, she'd need to make some more.

Deftly, she added another premeasured packet to the nest for coffee and poured in a cup's worth of water. The pot hissed merrily.

That ought to take care of the new arrival, she assured herself. Thank goodness Lillian had instructed her so well.

The minute she turned around there was another man at the door, this one short and stocky, far too compact to be an adequate swimmer. Without even waiting for the introduction, she added another pre-pack of coffee and more water to the reservoir. Drake certainly had a good many friends on the island. She found that admirable. But it didn't look like she'd have much chance to query James about the Salmon Woman with all these other men crowding into the room.

The coffeepot finally stopped hissing and dripping.

By now, in order to make room around the table, Matt was sitting on Drake's lap, a miniature replica of his father. His dark eyes were big and wide as he took in the conversation.

"Do you want something to drink, small-fry?" she asked.

"I'll have coffee, too," he announced. His chest puffed out in masculine bravado.

"You will not!" Drake dug his fingers into the boy's midsection until he squealed in delight. "Orange juice for little chip."

Dutifully, Aria found a glass for the juice and five cups for the coffee. After serving Matt, she placed a filled mug in front of Drake and each of his guests, and set one on the counter for herself.

She watched proudly as, in unison, the men took a sip of the brew.

Their eyes widened and four very manly faces turned bright red an instant before a chorus of choking and coughing filled the room.

"WERE YOU TRYING to kill us?"

The moment Aria had realized she'd made a terrible mistake, she'd fled the house and raced to her cabin up on the bluff. To her dismay Drake had followed her. And he hadn't taken no for an answer when he'd pounded on her door.

She lifted her chin in a mock show of defiance. "Of course not."

"That stuff was so potent, it'd melt stainless steel, not to mention what it'd do to a man's gut."

"I only did what Lillian told me. She promised the coffee would be perfect."

"Lillian's coffee has been known to grow hair on a man's chest. Yours burned it off." His dark brows lowered into a daunting line. "From the inside out."

Against her will, her gaze dropped to his chest. An intriguing tuft of dark hair peeked out above the circle of his undershirt. It appeared whatever damage she'd done to the growth of his chest hair had been minimal. She was relieved about that. "You didn't have to yell at me so loud. How was I supposed to know I'd put too much coffee in the pot?"

"You could have read the directions."

Slowly she raised her gaze to meet his again. She refused to flinch under his dark-eyed scrutiny. "I don't know how to read." Mermaids, after all, rarely had a need.

"You don't?"

"Is that a crime among your people?"

Something about his expression softened, the hard angles and planes of his rugged face mellowing with a touch of compassion. "I'm sorry, Aria. I didn't mean to embarrass you. I never would have guessed."

"Where I come from, no one learns to read."

"There aren't any schools?"

"Schools?" Puzzled by his odd question, she shook her head. "Not any that teach reading."

Drake speared his fingers through his hair without any particular intent to comb it. He felt like a fool for losing his temper with Aria, when it was no fault of her own that she couldn't read a few simple directions on a can of coffee. But he'd already been on the brink of a blowup because half the single men on the island had shown up to check Aria out—including a guy who probably ate more oysters than anyone else in the northern gulf. Not that he expected Joe Voulgan's performance would be all that great, with or without the help of a bucket of oysters.

Jealousy, he realized, had never been his style. Until now.

As he stared into the fascinating sea green of Aria's eyes, he had the oddest feeling the rental cabin had grown smaller and she was standing much closer to him now than she had been before. He wasn't sure if she had moved. Or if he had. The two narrow cots in the room faded from his awareness. So did the chest of drawers and stand-alone shower. Instead, her subtle fragrance filled his nostrils like the freshness of a summer's day wafting on an ocean breeze, tangy and sweet, capable of luring a man across the Pacific to an island paradise.

"Maybe you could study with Matt. He's just learning to read." His voice felt thick in his throat, the words not those he wanted to say. *I'd like to get to know you a whole lot better.* "As long as you're going to be here for a while."

"I think I'd like that." Her fingertips caressed the hollow of his throat as though she was trying to smooth away the lump there. It didn't work.

"Matt would probably like to have somebody to study with. Sometimes he gets bored."

A smile played at the corners of her lips and danced in her eyes as her fingers twined through the bit of hair she'd discovered. "I'm rarely bored."

"I can see that." Sweat beaded Drake's forehead. Lightning reactions pulsed through the rest of his body, as images flashed through his mind of just how "unboring" she could probably be. "We should start with the basics, though."

"I learn quickly. If I have the right teacher." Her fingertips left his throat to explore his chin.

His whiskers rasped beneath her sensual caress. There were an amazing number of things he'd like to teach her. Starting soon. "If you learn faster than we expect, we can always move on to more advanced studies." The ultimate home study course.

For one heated moment, her fingers touched his lower lip, then quickly withdrew. He caught her hand in his before she could escape. Through her porcelain skin, her bones felt as fragile as the wings of a sea bird. He'd forgotten how soft and vulnerable a woman could feel.

Like a whirlpool, the depth of her eyes drew him irresistibly into their vortex.

"Aria, I—"

"Teach me," she whispered. Standing on her tiptoes, she placed her lips on his, brazen and oddly innocent all at once—doubly sensual because of the strange juxtaposition of those two qualities.

Drake wasn't sure what happened in that next instant. He simply took what was offered, tasting the sweet flavor of her mouth, ravenous with all the pent-up hunger that had been driving him crazy since Aria had come into his life.

She answered his kiss with a gasp of pleasure that sent a shudder of longing through him. She wrapped her arms around his neck, drawing him closer, and he knew he was lost. Lost in the play of her tongue against his.

Awareness jerked through his body.

His senses reeled as he tried to regain his mental footing. The sensation staggered him, like trying to ride a ship on a breaching wave.

He didn't know anything about this woman, a woman who harbored secrets she wasn't willing to share. A stranger who had insinuated herself into his life. Hands shaking, he took her gently by the shoulders and stepped back.

Aria looked up in surprise and felt a shocking wave of despair. She'd initiated the kiss, but she'd had no idea what she'd been asking for. Not really. His lips and tongue had built a sweet, hot ache within her like none she'd ever felt. In contrast, the chill that now fell between them was like the coldest depths of the Arctic Ocean. Sterile. Devoid of life.

She hadn't understood what power she would unleash in Drake. Her body had melted under his potent masculinity. Rules for this exchange were unclear to her, goals muddled, while her mind tried—and failed—to keep up with the signals that darted in a frenzy of confusion to each cell in her body.

She wanted Drake Hart in a way she hadn't thought possible. Nor did she understand it.

"I think we'd better keep our relationship strictly business." A muscle ticked at Drake's jaw. "You're supposed to watch Matt and help out around the marina. If you want to sit in on Matt's studies, it's okay with me. I've got to get back to the guys. The way you ran out of the kitchen... I wanted to make sure you were all right."

He released her, and she found her new legs were as wobbly as the first time she'd tried them. Her heart, it seemed, was equally out of rhythm with the rapid rotation of the earth.

If this was her reaction to a simple kiss, clearly she'd have to rethink what it might mean to receive the milt of a human male—particularly if that male was Drake Hart.

A FEW DAYS LATER, as afternoon drove the clouds away, Drake was still trying to forget Aria's kiss—and not doing a very good job of it. He squatted on the roof of the toolshed, laying new asphalt shingles over the old ones. A weak sun had been playing peekaboo through a mostly overcast sky all day.

Matt scrambled up the ladder. "Hey, Dad—"

"Careful, son," Drake automatically warned. "These shingles are slippery."

The boy halted near the top of the ladder and hung his arms through the rung that was at chin level. "Can Aria come with me to Tiger Cubs tonight?"

"I don't think she'd be interested in your club meeting, son."

"But I need her to pin my badge on, D-Dad. It's my first b-badge and my mom's supposed to do it."

"You don't have a mother, son. I'll take care of it." Drake had been both mother and father to his son since the boy was in diapers. Pinning a badge on Matt didn't sound like a particularly difficult job.

"No, you don't understand," Matt pleaded. "Lil said she'd do it but she's gone. So Aria's g-gotta be my mom for tonight."

"Maybe you can borrow Tommy's mother. Alice would..." Drake's voice trailed off in the face of the tears that sprang into his son's eyes. He put down his hammer and worked his way across the roof to the ladder. He hadn't realized Matt was so troubled by not having a mother. It seemed to Drake like they were getting along fine without a full-time woman in their lives. "If it's that important, son, I guess we can ask Aria."

A victorious smile creased a dimple in Matt's cheek. "I already d-did. She said she'd go if it was okay with you."

Now why, Drake wondered, did he feel like he'd just been conned by his own son?

THEY ATE an early dinner and then got into Drake's vehicle, which he had parked near the cabins. Aria found traveling on land even more unsettling than sailing over the top of the water in his boat. In the fading late-afternoon sun, the scenery raced by in a blur. Sudden dips in the road jarred her and she held on tight to the door handle.

She glanced nervously at Drake. Sweet Neptune, if riding in a car was this frightening, flying in Chuck's plane might well terrify her right out of her skin! Assuming he remembered having once made the offer.

To distract herself, Aria asked Matt, "You didn't

tell me why the Tiger Cubs are giving you a badge of honor."

"It's a Good Citizen Award." Sitting in the back seat, he leaned forward between Drake and Aria. He had on a dark blue uniform shirt and a yellow tie. His hair had been slicked back so there wasn't a single strand out of place. He looked quite adorable and ever so serious. "All us T-Tiger Cubs picked up litter down by the ferry landing. Bags and bags of it."

"They did a good job," Drake assured her. He'd cleaned up, too, and was freshly shaved. The shirt he'd chosen was the shade of a tropical lagoon and made a striking contrast to his dark brown eyes.

"And then I had to clean my room all by myself."

Drake's lips quirked. "He discovered toys buried in that swamp that he hadn't seen since he was two years old."

"D-Dad!"

Stifling a laugh, Aria gave the boy an encouraging smile. "I'm sure you did a fine job."

"Then I had to do three g-good deeds. Lil helped me think of stuff."

"My gracious, it sounds like you certainly deserve the badge. I'll be very honored to pin it on you." On the other hand, Aria was quite anxious about all the people who would be at the village community center Matt had described. She definitely wasn't comfortable in large groups and was afraid she would say or do something that might give away her secret.

As Drake took a turn at particularly high speed, Aria's stomach fluttered nervously. She did hope she wouldn't embarrass Matt or his father tonight.

AFTER PARKING his Jeep in the vacant lot beside the community center, Drake escorted Aria and Matt inside. He noticed the speculative glances of the other parents, most of whom he'd known since he'd been Matt's age. Trying to avoid too many questions, he ushered Aria to the cookie and punch table while Matt joined his fellow Tiger Cubs for the ceremony.

"So many people," Aria whispered as he handed her a cup of punch. Her hand trembled slightly.

He shrugged, puzzled that she seemed nervous. About fifteen families were milling around, hardly a big gathering in his view. When everyone on the island got together for summer fish fries, two or three hundred people filled the small village to overflowing, and that included tourists.

Alice Kelly hurried up to the table with a plate of sugar cookies in her hands. "Don't the boys look adorable in their little uniforms?" she said breathlessly. She was one of those women who had taken to motherhood like a duck to water. Unfortunately, the birth of three children had added several inches around her waist since her high school cheerleading days, but she didn't seem to mind. Drake figured her husband was a lucky guy. "I thought we'd never get Tommy's tie right. Is Lil going to pin Matt's badge on?"

"No, ah, Aria is." He quickly introduced the two women. "Aria is filling in around the marina and watching Matt for me while Lil's visiting her daughter."

"Oh, how nice. Here, have one of these." Alice extended the plate of cookies toward Aria.

Smiling brightly, Aria selected one. "Hmm, sand dollars! They look delicious. My mother used to bleach sand dollars on the rocks till they were just this color and extra chewy." She glanced around the room distractedly. "Of course, the gulls always tried to steal them from her."

Alice gave Drake an incredulous look. "They're sugar cookies."

"I know," he mumbled.

Aria had the cookie halfway to her mouth before she realized she'd said something stupid. Again. She'd been so nervous and uncomfortable about the curious stares she'd been receiving, she hadn't been thinking, and the words had simply slipped out. Heat raced to her cheeks. She laughed self-consciously and tried to cover her mistake. "Of course, my mother loved to play jokes on us children. So do I."

"Yes, well…" Her smile fading, Alice glanced toward the front of the meeting room where there was a platform set up. "I think they're about ready to begin. I'll just go, ah…nice to meet you."

As Alice hurried across the room, Aria expelled a discouraged sigh. What must Drake's friend think of her? Obviously it was more complicated to fit into human society than to simply replace a tail with a pair of legs. That was a troubling thought, one she didn't want to examine too closely.

It seemed everyone in the room knew Drake and greeted him with a touch of deference, as if he were a young king whom they admired. She remembered the merpeople of her village treating her father in that same way.

In contrast, Aria felt uncomfortably like a fish out of water.

"Oh, look," she said as Drake was leading her to a couple of empty seats at the back of the room. "There's James, your friend from the lighthouse."

Drake nodded. "He's probably got a grandson in the Tiger Cubs."

"Maybe we'll have a chance to speak with him later?"

"Maybe," Drake said noncommittally.

Aria hoped so. She had yet to pursue James's comments about seeing a Salmon Woman. Discovering a community of salmon people might still be her best option for the future. Particularly if she couldn't get Drake to cooperate with the other alternative.

DRAKE SETTLED into a folding chair, troubled by the feeling that this was a family event and that he, Matt and Aria were imposters. She wasn't his wife—or Matt's mother. He was a single dad and that was just fine with him.

Or at least it was until Aria went up front with the other mothers. She made such a striking picture, with her long blond hair and delicate features, he couldn't keep his eyes off her. He watched a tentative smile play at the corners of her full lips when the Tiger Cub leader read off Matt's accomplishments. He wanted to kiss those lips again. Soon.

But when she knelt to pin Matt's badge to his shirt, Drake's throat tightened on a lump, and he had to swipe at his eyes with the back of his hand. Matt looked so darn proud of himself, and Aria beamed the boy the gentlest, most loving smile Drake had ever seen. It made him ache for something that went way beyond lust and was a hell of a lot more difficult to ease.

After the ceremony was over, Matt came running through the crowd.

"Hey, Dad, did you see Aria and m-me?"

"Sure did, little chip." He cupped the back of the boy's head.

"She did good, didn't she, Dad?"

"Just fine, son. So did you."

Matt tugged on his arm so he would bend over. "Do you think maybe someday she could be my *real* mom?" he whispered.

Drake choked on a sudden cough. "I'd have to think about that for a while, son."

"How long?" he insisted.

Looking up, Drake was snared by a pair of intriguing sea green eyes. Since when had his son started matchmaking? And how come Drake couldn't manage to reject the idea out of hand?

He was still trying to understand his reaction to Matt's suggestion three days later as he was checking the rental fishing tackle and old reels.

He'd made a valiant effort to ignore Aria since the Tiger Cub ceremony and all the emotions her participation had generated in him about home and family. It wasn't easy. *Impossible* came closer to the truth.

Every time he turned around, she'd done something nice for either him or Matt. Like the seashell belt she'd made for the kid. Or the way she'd sewn up a ripped hip pocket on an old pair of his jeans—after he'd shown her how to thread a needle.

She'd even been learning with Matt's help to cook a decent meal. Sort of.

But still he tried to keep his distance.

He'd been working all morning repairing equipment. The air was damp with the threat of rain, the wind blustery. He figured a cup of coffee—one he made himself—would take the chill away.

As he entered the house through the back door, he heard talking in the living room. The sound of Aria's voice, as sweet and bright as sunlight bursting through the clouds on a winter day, slowed his steps. The lyrical notes seeped through the shield he'd built around himself and touched a tender spot deep inside, warming him in a way coffee never could.

He hadn't realized how much he'd missed the

sweet gentleness a woman could bring to a man's home.

Drawn across the room like a hungry fish lured by a particularly tempting bit of bait, he listened to Aria talking with Matt.

"Is it hard to learn the alphabet?" she asked.

"Uh-uh. See, there's big letters and little letters. The big ones are the easiest to learn."

"Then I should probably start with those."

Drake felt a twinge of guilt that he hadn't been helping Aria learn to read, as he had promised. But you had to be in the same room with someone to teach them, and he'd been avoiding being that close to Aria.

"The *A* comes first," Matt explained. "It looks like a big ol' fir tree. Like this." Matt paused and his pencil scratched the letter on a piece of paper. "Then comes *B*. It's like a fat guy with two big bellies."

"Two bellies! Goodness."

"Then there's *C*. It's like a clam with its mouth wide open."

"Oh, yes. I can see that." Her laughter sprinkled the air like raindrops dimpling the water on a windless day.

As Drake continued to eavesdrop, he realized an amazing thing was happening. Matt wasn't stuttering. He hadn't blocked on a single word since Drake had been standing there.

Wondering if that meant the boy was finally outgrowing his speech problem, Drake went to make coffee, only to discover there was already some in the pot. He eyed it critically. With the caution born of experience, he poured a little into a mug and sipped it gingerly. Not bad.

Filling the mug, he carried it into the living room. The student and her young tutor were sitting on the floor in front of the coffee table, Buffy curled up between them, her head resting on Aria's foot.

"Sounds like you're turning into a pretty good schoolteacher, son."

Matt's head snapped up. "Aria's real s-smart."

"So are you, Matt," Aria insisted. "You are very young to already know so much."

"My d-dad taught me."

Squatting down at the coffee table next to his son, Drake suddenly wondered if there was something about him that caused Matt to stutter. He didn't like to consider that possibility. "So how far have you gotten in the alphabet?"

"I'm showing her *I* now." He laboriously wrote the capital letter next to a slightly tilted *H*, two men shaking hands. "My d-dad says an *I* looks like a lighthouse."

Aria glanced at Drake. "Like the lighthouse where your friend James works?"

"Sort of. I thought comparing the letters to what he already knows would help Matt remember better."

"I remember all the stuff you taught me. See? *J* is a fish hook."

"That's right, son." Smiling, Drake ruffled the boy's hair.

"Is the lighthouse somewhere nearby?" Aria asked.

"About a mile south of here at the tip of the island. The dirt road we took into the village goes past the lighthouse in the opposite direction. Most of the time it's passable only with four-wheel drive. James has an old truck he drives like a dragster. Tries to set a new speed record every time he gets behind the wheel."

Aria nodded, pleased to know how to reach the lighthouse and that it wasn't far. She was anxious to learn more about the Salmon Woman that James had seen, but found her travels severely limited by being forced to rely on legs rather than swimming. Her usual method of transportation was much faster and would have allowed her to circle the entire island, if need be, to discover the whereabouts of the lighthouse.

She regretted she'd missed her chance to speak to James at the Tiger Cub ceremony, but he'd been gone by the time she looked for him again.

"*K-K* is like a man strutting."

Aria shifted her thoughts back to the alphabet lesson and her young teacher. "Strutting?"

"Yeah, I'll show you." Matt hopped up and marched around the room, snapping his arms and legs stiffly back and forth in an exaggerated motion.

"I see." Amused, she stroked Buffy's head. In

turn, the cat licked her hand with a determined tongue.

"It was the best I could come up with when he was learning the alphabet," Drake mumbled.

Her lips quirked in amusement. "I'm quite certain I'll never forget a *K* with such a vivid demonstration."

"Wait till you get to *X* and *Y*."

She raised her brows. "I'll look forward to it."

Matt made three full strutting circles around the room, each one at an increasing speed until he was nearly running. Drake said, "That's enough, kid. Lessons are over for now."

"Can I go outside? C-can I?"

"For now, you can. We're gonna get rain later."

"We *always* get rain."

"Don't forget your jacket."

Scowling at the parental reminder, Matt stomped into the kitchen. A moment later the back door slammed.

"He'll be all right by himself?" Aria asked.

"He's fine. I've drilled safety rules into him since he could crawl." Drake leaned back against the couch and sighed. "The problem is his attention span isn't very long yet, particularly for schoolwork. He's like a baby whale who stays underwater too long. When he surfaces, he blows higher than any adult can handle."

"He's a delightful little boy. You've done well raising him on your own."

"It hasn't always been easy." He picked up the

pencil from the table and wove it through his fingers. "You're good with him. He doesn't even stutter when he's with you."

"I've noticed."

"Maybe I've put too much pressure on him and that's why he's having trouble."

"No. Don't blame yourself."

"Maybe if his mother had stuck around..."

"Do you still miss her?"

"I knew within the first three months that she was too young to settle down, and we'd both made a mistake by getting married. I hadn't known her for very long—she'd come to the island to work during the tourist season. It turned out we didn't have anything in common." Except hot sex, he admitted to himself. That wasn't enough to carry a marriage, particularly when he'd begun to suspect Janie was hopping in and out of every guy's bed from here to the mainland. At the time, he'd felt a terrible sense of betrayal, like he'd been blindsided. He still felt the same way. "I tried to make it work, but she wanted me to sell the marina and move to Vancouver or Seattle. She wanted to be where the action was."

"You didn't want to go?"

He tossed the pencil onto the table and it rolled to the opposite side. "Leaving Hart's Cove would be like voluntarily cutting off my right leg. I couldn't do that."

"Functioning with only one good leg would be difficult," she conceded. She picked up the pencil and traced the letter *I* Matt had drawn for her. It seemed to stand for both the strength of a lighthouse and the rigid determination of a man like Drake. She could empathize with his desire to remain in the home where he'd grown up and failed to understand why any woman would want him to leave. Had it not been for Oceana, Aria would still be enjoying the comfort of familiar waters.

"The only good thing that came out of my marriage was Matt. He was worth all the grief."

A rush of hope raised Aria's head. Perhaps all she needed was to explain her need to get pregnant and he would be willing to cooperate. "Then you'd like more children?"

His eyes narrowed. "I'm a confirmed bachelor, Aria. I jumped to a rash decision once and I've learned my lesson. I'm not planning to enlarge my family anytime soon and not without a hell of a lot of thought first."

She gritted her teeth in frustration and disappointment. *Soon* was exactly when she needed to act. The days were drifting by far too rapidly. Except for sharing meals together, Drake had obviously been avoiding her. His unwillingness to share his milt was downright selfish in her view.

A ripple of rising panic resonated along her spine. If Drake couldn't, or *wouldn't,* help her, she'd have to find some other alternative. If only Oceana hadn't been so determined to ban her from her school of merpeople, she wouldn't be faced with this life-threatening dilemma. She'd still be cavorting with her friends in warm tropical waters. If only...

A shuddering sigh escaped her lips.

She'd simply have to slip away that afternoon to visit the lighthouse. If James could lead her to the salmon people, she might still manage to survive the winter in these northern waters, where she would eventually be transformed into a mermaid again during the next full moon.

"SHE WAS DOWN THERE, just off the point." James pointed down the rocky slope where it extended out into the straits. Water swirled over hidden boulders, retreating as the tide went out to meet the treacherous currents that scoured the south end of the island. Gulls dipped and soared, diving into the eddies when they spotted a tasty morsel suitable for a meal. Then, eating their catch, they perched on the pilings that formed a wooden dock for James's runabout boat.

"Are you sure what you saw was the Salmon Woman?" Aria asked, sending up a quick prayer to the gods of the sea that she could yet find a home for herself.

"The night was as dark as pitch, but I know what I saw. I've got my light." He thumbed up to the beacon on top of the lighthouse. It rotated in a familiar sweep of white light to warn sailors—and wary merpeople—away from dangerous shoals.

"She had hair that looked like silver seaweed in the light," he said. "Miles of it floating behind her.

I wasn't sure at first what I was seeing, then she raised her tail like I've seen sea bass do when they get into a school of smelt and go a little crazy. Beautiful sight, it was.''

"Could it actually have been a sea bass and you imagined—"

"Not a chance, little lady." He laughed. The breeze caught a few strands of his gray hair and whipped them across his face. "I'm not so old I don't remember what a beautiful woman looks like.''

"Would you mind…could I go down there closer to the water?''

"Of course you can. But mind your step. Those rocks can be slippery, and I don't imagine young Drake would appreciate it if I had to rescue you if you fell in.''

"I'll be careful." Though she still missed her tail, each day she grew more confident using her legs and thought she could handle the uneven surface of boulders. The walk to the lighthouse had been quite pleasant, filled with the sight of interesting land animals and plants she'd never before viewed so closely. The lush scent of the forest had nearly masked the more familiar fragrance of the sea and was, in its own way, equally appealing.

Moving with care, she made her way down to the water's edge. She dipped her hand into the frigid sea.

Unlike the waters around Sechelt, there was life here, a busy community of crustaceans, smelts, squid and the fish that preyed on them. But she sensed nothing large enough to be the Salmon Woman James had described. Perhaps she had moved on, taking with her Aria's last chance to find people of her own kind.

Tears stung at the back of her eyes and she let the wind wipe them away. Never had she felt so alone, not even when her mother had died. Then she'd had a loving father to console her. But now... Fear tightened her throat. If only Drake would share his milt...

She made her way up the boulders to where James was waiting for her.

"Pretty spot, isn't it?" he said.

"Yes, it's lovely." The whole island was beautiful, as well as the sea around it.

"Couple of funny things about the Salmon Woman." He jammed his hands into the pockets of his heavy jacket.

"What's that?"

"First off, I would of guessed she'd have black hair, not blond, her being part of an Indian legend."

"Maybe it was just the way your light was shining on her hair that made you think it was a light color."

"Could be," he conceded, looking thoughtfully out toward the straits. "I could have sworn I heard her singing, too. In fact, I came out here to get a closer look, and I had this terrible urge to climb down those rocks and maybe follow her right into the sea."

"Why is that so unusual?"

"Never once, not in all the times I've heard the legend of the Salmon Woman, have I ever heard a storyteller say she could sing. It's a sound this ol' man will never forget, you can be sure of that."

Aria went very still. "Did you feel like she was *luring* you into the ocean?"

"Yep. She wanted me, all right. I know that sounds like I'm as crazy as a seasick tuna fish, but that's how I felt. And I'll tell you one thing, my heart was willing but my body sure couldn't manage. Not anymore."

A shiver of anxiety sped down Aria's spine. *Mermaids* lured sailors into the sea to drown. It didn't appear that tales of the Salmon Woman included that antihuman behavior. But the one mermaid Aria knew who had long, flowing blond hair and thrived on enticing men to follow her to their deaths was Oceana, her stepmother.

Aria scanned the dark reaches of the straits. Was it possible Oceana had followed her this far? And if she had, why would she have done so?

Wrapping her arms around her midsection, Aria pulled her jacket tight to ward off the chill air. She needed to get home—to Drake and his son—and make sure they were safe.

Chapter Six

Drake glanced up at the sound of Aria hurrying down the slope from the cabins. She was all but sailing down the path, as graceful as a seabird but looking far more troubled, a frown tugging at her forehead. Her hair glistened with the first few drops of rain—diamonds on silver-blond curls.

"What's wrong?" he asked when she reached him.

She drew several deep gulps of air. "Are you all right?"

"Sure. Why wouldn't I be?"

"And Matt?"

"He and I have been practicing casting. He's getting pretty good." Though their success had been limited to catching a few shiners. He'd hoped for better, given Aria's far more impressive luck from the end of the dock.

"Thank the old man of the sea!" she said with a sigh.

Drake frowned. "What did you expect?"

"Oh, nothing. Nothing at all." Her shoulders

sagged with what appeared to be relief. What the hell was this woman hiding? "I'll just go check on Matt."

"He's fine." Drake snared her arm before she could get away. "The local police stopped by while you were gone."

"Oh?" She looked at him blankly. *Innocently.*

"Willy tells me there's a woman missing from Nanaimo. No one has seen her for several days." Not since the night Aria had washed up on his shore. "They found her car parked down by the ferry dock, but there's been no other sign of her. And no one remembers seeing her on the ferry."

"I hope she's all right. Is she someone you know?"

"You tell me, Aria. They say she's about five foot two and has long, blond hair."

Her forehead wrinkled into a puzzled frown.

"According to the police, her name is Susan Willcox. Does that name sound familiar to you?"

She shook her head. "I don't think so."

"Word is, her husband is bad news. The neighbors claim his favorite hobby was beating the tar out of her. They figure she might have run away." Lifting his hand, Drake caressed Aria's soft cheek. The cut she'd had on her forehead was only a faint scar now. It tore at his gut to think that some man might have done that to her—especially a man who was her husband. "Or it's possible he killed her and dumped her off the ferry landing."

"Oh, my, that's terrible! I hope she ran away and

is a thousand leagues from here by now. No man ought to hit his wife. It shouldn't happen.''

"I agree, in spades. And Aria, if you ever need help, or need to keep out of the clutches of some bozo who wants to use you for a punching bag, you can count on me. I'll keep you safe. I promise.''

"That's very sweet of you, Drake.'' She leaned her cheek into his palm, pressing his rough calluses into her soft flesh. "But I don't think there's much likelihood of that happening.''

"Well, I wanted you to know. In case you were ever…well, if you ever had that kind of a problem.''

"Thank you.'' She stood on tiptoe and gave him a fleeting kiss. "I'm going to go check on Matt. Just to be sure—''

She whirled and ran back up the dock, leaving Drake staring after her, admiring the rhythmic sway of her hips and wondering what was going on in that clever little head of hers. She hadn't reacted as if she were the missing Nanaimo woman. But Willy's description was certainly a match. He'd said he would be getting a photo soon and would bring it around for Drake to look at and maybe ID. It would certainly explain Aria's secretive attitude if she was hiding out from an abusive husband.

Drake shoved his fists into his jacket. If the guy showed up at Hart's Cove and threatened Aria, Drake would damn well guarantee he'd never lay a hand on her. Never again.

Perversely—in spite of everything that he'd

vowed—he hated the fact that she might be married to some other man.

BY THE NEXT MORNING, a high-pressure ridge had pushed the clouds and rain south, promising a sunny day for the first time in more than a week. The timing was perfect for Drake's charter clients. Now all he had to do was find some trophy catches for them somewhere within several thousand square miles of water that was notorious for giving up its bounty grudgingly.

He wolfed down the last of his breakfast cereal and drained his mug of coffee.

"How come I can't g-go with you, Dad?"

"Not this time, son. These are important clients and I've got to concentrate on making their trip perfect so they'll come back again. They want to catch their limit."

"But, D-Dad—" Matt whined.

"You stay here with Aria. I'll take you out on the boat one day next week. I promise."

"Ah, gee…"

Aria picked up Drake's empty bowl and set it in the sink along with those left over from dinner. "If it is important that these clients of yours catch so many fish, perhaps I should go with you."

"Thanks, anyway, but some men don't like to have women along when they're fishing." Though with Aria on board she might distract the guys so much they wouldn't even remember why they were on the boat—a situation that did have a certain amount of merit if the fishing didn't go well.

"I could locate the fish for you," Aria said. "All you'd have to do is catch them. I can even tell you what they're feeding on so you can use the right bait."

Shoving back from the table, he gave her a disbelieving look. "I've been fishing all my life and I can't always find fish, even with an electronic detector. What makes you think you can?"

She smiled smugly. "It's a talent I have. Like catching fish by tickling their tummies."

"She does that real good, Dad. You seen her."

He shot Matt a silencing look. It didn't work.

"So, since Aria has gotta go fishing with you, that means I get to g-go, too."

"You can go to Tommy's house if Mrs. Kelly says she doesn't mind."

"Yeah? All right!" He pumped his fist in the air in a victory salute, evidently deciding playing with Tommy would be a lot more fun than hanging around with his old man.

Drake grabbed his jacket from the rack and pulled it on, almost as surprised as Matt at the impulsive decision he'd just made. He didn't normally like to bother Alice Kelly with looking after Matt, nor did he usually take other passengers along on a charter trip. But this time...

"It'd be a long day on the boat for you, Matt, and you'd be bored to death. Aria can..." Drake didn't want to admit that maybe she did have some magic skill at finding fish. Or that he liked the idea of her coming along simply because he wanted to be near her. "I can always use a little help in the galley. Aria can make coffee and sandwiches for the men when they get hungry."

Her finely arched eyebrows shot up. "You want me to make coffee for your clients?"

"You've been getting better at it." The corners of his mouth twitched with the threat of a smile. "Besides, something that potent will keep their minds off their troubles if we don't catch anything."

"We will," she said, folding her arms across her chest, her eyes sparking at his challenge.

As soon as Drake left to take Matt to his friend's house, Aria scurried around to get herself ready. She stared at the pile of dishes in the sink, most of them left from dinner last night and thoroughly stuck with the remnants of supper. She sighed as she glanced at the breakfast dishes still sitting on the table. There really wasn't enough time to wash all of them and put them away before Drake returned. All that washing and scrubbing seemed like an odd custom, in any event. Merpeople simply used whatever shell was handy as they needed it and then tossed it away. A very practical procedure when the sea was filled with all the shells anyone could possibly want.

She didn't dare not be ready to leave when Drake was. He might decide to go off without her. And she wasn't sure it was safe for Drake to be out fishing without her to protect him—and was grateful

Matt would be out of harm's way staying at his friend's house.

Since she'd talked with James, she'd grown increasingly concerned that he had seen Oceana, not the legendary Salmon Woman. In fact, late last night she'd been almost sure she'd heard her stepmother's voice calling into the darkness. But the distance had been too great for her to be positive. The wind and rain humming through the trees might have accounted for the sound.

But Aria didn't want to take any chances. As wicked as Oceana was, she'd have no more scruples about harming a child than a grown man.

With a few hurried trips, she took the dishes from the sink and shoved them into the oven. Then she added the bowls and glasses from the table, slammed the door shut and wiped the counter clean. There'd be plenty of time after the fishing trip to wash dishes, a chore she had not yet learned to relish even though Drake seemed to think it was important.

Perhaps she should teach him to use shells instead of plates.

She'd just gotten everything organized in the kitchen when she heard Drake's footsteps on the dock.

"Ready, Aria?" he shouted.

"Coming." Grabbing her jacket, she dashed out the door and ran down the dock.

The early morning sunlight streaked through a fine mist that rose from the water, creating rainbows of glistening color. Flocks of small birds skimmed only feet above the surface. They darted this way and that, finally deciding as of one mind to soar higher, parting the mist and finding a noisy perch on the trees that lined the shore.

Aria wondered how anyone could possibly tire of such an incredible scene.

"Grab the bowline, then hop aboard," Drake ordered. Exhaust from the idling engine mixed with the rising mist, and the hum of the motor provided a low counterpoint to the high-pitched calls of the birds.

Feeling more lighthearted than she had in a long while, in spite of her concern about Oceana, Aria smiled and waved to Drake.

He smiled back.

A big, broad grin creased his cheek and did something extraordinary to her insides—something wild, private and very feminine.

She wanted to leap up and wave her tail in the air. And nearly got her legs tangled together thinking about it.

With more spirit than grace, she clambered aboard, the bow now free of its tether to the dock.

"I'll make a sailor out of you yet," he said with a low chuckle.

She thought that unlikely but didn't bother to correct him.

Drake added power, and the boat edged away from the dock. Standing at the helm, he looked every inch the captain of the ship. His brown leather jacket hung open. Beneath it, a soft plaid shirt in shades of brown and green tugged across a flat belly.

"We're picking up the clients at Sechelt," he told her. "They've got their wives with them, and they wanted to stay at a place a little classier than my cabins."

"I think your cabins are nice. The bed is very comfortable."

He slanted her a curious look as though he wanted to challenge her statement. "I'll be sure to put your three-star recommendation in my next advertising brochure."

Aria wasn't sure what he meant but it didn't matter. She liked being here with Drake, leaving the sheltered harbor and racing across the glassy calm water with the wind blowing in her face. She liked a lot of things about being human, particularly the feelings she got when Drake looked at her in that special, curious way.

Or when he smiled especially for her.

He'd shaved that morning, and his cheeks looked smooth. In the bright sunlight he squinted. His expressive brows were lowered, and little lines were apparent at the corners of his dark eyes. Her fingers itched to touch him. She wanted to explore the firm line of his jaw, the arch of the intriguing brows. Mostly she wanted to investigate once again the thrill of his lips on hers.

And share his milt.

She sighed and looked out across the quiet water, searching for the telltale lift of a silver tail that would mean a very large fish—or an average-size mermaid—was swimming nearby. Nothing broke the surface, not even a young albacore coming up to look around.

"Was Alice Kelly unhappy about watching Matt for the day?" Aria asked, even as she kept an eye out for any unusual signs in the water.

"No. In fact, she said there's no hurry to pick him up. She's not working now because of the slow tourist season and seemed happy enough to have Matt around for her boy to play with."

"You're fortunate to have so many friends on the island."

"Like folks in most small towns, we watch out for each other."

Aria's merpeople village had been like that, too. Until Oceana arrived and deceived her father into marriage.

"Of course, all bets are off when it comes to fishing."

"Oh?"

He tossed her another teasing grin. "Chuck Lampert has a charter today, too. I'd like nothing better than for my guys to catch their limit—all big ones—and have Chuck come up empty."

"A friendly competition?"

"Heck, no. It's no holds barred when it comes to fishing—and women." He winked at her. "And let the better man win."

His good mood was contagious and she laughed along with him. Unable to resist, she smoothed his dark hair back from his forehead, the strands thick and silken to her touch. "I'll do my part. I promise."

"That's fine by me. Why don't you start by making a pot of coffee. We're almost there."

She scowled. Drake had no idea how efficient she was at finding fish. But if she had a chance, she'd prove her inborn talents exceeded any electronic invention that he had tucked up his sleeve.

JEROME AND BOB, loud-mouth former football players from Southern California, weren't Drake's favorite kind of clients, but they paid full price and tipped well, assuming the catch warranted it. Drake intended to see they got every bit of what they were willing and able to pay for.

"So how are we going to do today?" Jerome asked. He was the more blustery of the two and more overweight, his classic down jacket straining its zipper across a belly that had gone from muscle to fat. They'd just boarded and already he'd popped open a can of beer, even though it was still early morning.

"Let's get out into the main channel and then we'll take a look around," Drake told him. "Aria's got coffee ready for you below decks."

"She's a real looker," Bob said. "Where'd you find her?"

"Let's just say she's my deckhand, and I'm real protective of the people who work for me."

Bob shrugged noncommittally. "Hope she makes

good coffee. My wife is into designer coffee. It's wimpy as hell. Real men shouldn't have to drink French vanilla fru-fru or rootie-tootie expresso.''

Drake swallowed a laugh. ''If that's how you feel, I think you'll like Aria's coffee just fine.''

While the fishermen stowed their gear, Drake navigated toward the straits at full throttle. The best fishing was usually between Quadra Island and Vancouver Island where the waters narrowed and schooling fish packed together. He kept an eye out for floating logs that were always a threat to flip a fast-moving boat and stayed alert for other fishing craft. It didn't take him long to spot Lampert's boat heading toward the same fishing grounds.

''Let's hope Aria really is a secret weapon,'' he mumbled to himself. Or maybe his own lucky instincts would pay off this time, as they had so often in the past when he'd been looking to bring in a big catch.

Wheeling into the north-flowing current, he throttled back.

''Bait up, gentlemen,'' he called. ''Can't catch anything unless your lines are wet.''

Tugging his baseball cap firmly on his head, Bob tossed him a salute. ''You got it, cap'n.''

Drake switched on the fish finder. The screen flickered and then settled into a steady glow. In the deep channel, there was little bounce on the radar screen from the sea floor. There were also darn few signs of any fish.

The two fishermen dropped their live bait into the water and spun out their lines on silent reels.

"We'll drift awhile and see what we can pick up," he told Bob and Jerome, who had settled into the deck chairs at the stern of the boat.

"Should have had a hit by now," Jerome groused as he took another swig of beer.

"Shut up, Jerry," his partner said. "Give the man a chance."

The radar screen continued to appear discouragingly empty of anything worth catching. Drake eased the boat closer to the big island.

Aria came up from below deck and squinted in the bright sunshine. "Have they caught anything yet?"

"You and Jerome should learn a little patience," Drake muttered. "We'll find 'em."

She peered over his shoulder. "That's like Matt's TV. Is that how you find fish?"

"This device is a little more complicated than plugging in a videotape and costs a bundle more than any satellite dish. I can see a hundred feet down with this baby, and any fish that are moving will show up."

"Oh." The flickering green screen didn't look to Aria like it would find any fish. "But it only looks straight down?"

"More or less."

"Well, that's no way to find fish. They aren't likely to all swim right under your boat, are they?"

"This thing works," he objected. "There's nothing better."

Except her.

Aria walked to the back of the boat, climbed over the railing and knelt on the transom next to the bait tank. She slipped her hand into the water.

"What are you up to, little lady?" Jerome asked.

"I'm trying to find some fish for you to catch."

"That surely is nice of you, sweetheart, but don't you think you ought to leave that to us menfolk?"

Biting off a retort that might lose Drake his customers, she asked sweetly, "What sort of fish would you prefer catching today?"

"Honey, anything will do as long as you're smilin' at me."

"How about an albacore or two?" Bob suggested.

"There are only young ones in these waters."

"They're good fighters, though. If you and Drake can hook us into a couple of twenty inchers, we'll be happy."

Jerome shoved his elbow at Bob. "Hell, I wanna catch me a sea bass. Heard they got some big suckers up here. Maybe I could have it stuffed and mount the thing over my wife's bed." He hacked a laugh that lacked humor. "Bet she'd love it."

Grimacing, Aria doubted that.

Drake leaned over the railing. "Aria, I think you ought to come back on deck. I don't want you to fall overboard. That water's darn cold."

She gestured for him to lean closer. "There's a school of young albacore about five hundred yards off to our right," she whispered in his ear. "They're feeding on squid."

"How could you—" he sputtered. "They are?"

She nodded.

Drake looked at her skeptically. He knew it didn't make any sense that she could locate fish by simply dipping her hand in the water, much less that she'd know what kind of bait to use. But it wasn't reasonable she could tickle a fish's stomach, either. And he'd seen her do that. Or at least he'd seen the impressive results.

Right now, given a really blank screen on the fish finder, he didn't have any choice but to give Aria's advice a try.

"Gentlemen, let's reel in. I've got some artificial lures I think might work better than live bait this time."

She smiled up at him and Drake figured that smile was worth a hundred pounds of fish. Maybe more. Bob and Jerome be damned!

Within an hour they'd hauled in a half dozen hard-fighting albacore by cruising back and forth across the school. The radar screen was alive with big fish chasing little fish.

"There's no prettier sound than singing reels," Drake shouted when Bob hooked into one that stole a hundred feet of line in a matter of seconds. The nylon spun off the reel with a high-pitched zing.

After a while two other boats showed up to piggyback on their success, Lampert's boat included.

But by that time the fish had been spooked and the pickings were lean.

Drake tried not to gloat. Much.

The trolling lines were quiet when Aria reported, "There're some sea bass north of us. None seem very big but Jerome wants a trophy. I've told him—"

"A man like Jerome doesn't listen real well." Drake linked his arm around Aria's waist and pulled her close. The bulky sweatshirt she was wearing was soft and cuddly; the leotard pants revealed every perfect curve of calf and thigh. Her unique scent of sunshine and sea mixed with the salt in the air and Drake inhaled deeply. "I don't know how you did it, but you were right on with those albacore. If you say there's sea bass up there, we'll give it a try."

Without releasing his hold on Aria, he edged the throttle forward. She snuggled up to him. A woman who could find fish by simply putting her fingertips in the water would make a hell of a good business partner for a man who ran a charter service.

He tried to set the thought aside, but it persisted, settling at the back of his mind like a dream that refused to go away. He'd made a mistake thinking after only a few weeks of knowing Janie that she would be a helpmate in his business. He knew of no reason to suspect his snap judgments about people, particularly women, had improved over the years. But still, the possibility lingered at the fringes of his awareness.

They reached the narrows and began a slow troll

of the waters. In short order, both Bob and Jerome landed a couple of small sea bass. That didn't satisfy Jerome.

"Come on, Drake, ol' buddy. You can do better than this. Find us some *big* ones!"

Drake liked catching trophy fish as much as anybody—maybe more. But they didn't leap out of the water on demand. You had to work at it and have plenty of luck on your side.

He checked his fish finder, which was dotted with medium size fish, but nothing worth writing home about. Then he asked Aria, "You got any ideas?"

"The currents are very turbulent here. It's hard to read these waters, but I think farther up the narrows there may be larger fish feeding."

"This is pretty calm compared to when there's a tidal exchange going on," Drake told her. "Then you can get tidal streams running through here at up to sixteen knots. If the surge is bad enough, whirlpools actually show up." He'd nearly been caught in one once. An experience he wouldn't want to repeat.

"That sounds dangerous."

"It is," he said grimly. "A lot of boats have been swallowed up in these narrows."

"Then maybe we shouldn't risk it."

A quick glance at his watch told Drake the tide would begin to turn in about an hour. Not much time to locate and land a respectable haul of fish.

"Come on, Drake," Jerome chided him. "You're supposed to be a top guide. Maybe next time we oughta go with Lampert. They tell me he's got one hell of a rep.''

The threat shot through Drake like the shaft of a harpoon, and his competitive juices surged. "I'll get you the trophy you want. Just hang on to your hats.''

Chapter Seven

Aria clung to the boat railing. The men were having a grand time landing one handsome sea bass after another. She wasn't having fun at all. Not now. Even with her feet planted firmly on the deck, she could sense the tide shifting.

"We'd better go," she warned Drake.

He checked his watch and scanned the shoreline. "In a few minutes. I'd like to give Jerome a chance to catch one more. That'll shut him up about going out with Lampert next time."

"He's already caught three. So has Bob. Isn't that enough?"

"I'll give it just a minute more."

Stubborn man, particularly when his competitive spirit had been tweaked. She gritted her teeth and tried to will some hapless sea bass onto Jerome's hook so they could all leave these dangerous waters.

"Fish on!" he yelled.

Aria's head snapped around. Jerome's pole was nearly bent in half; his taut line pulled almost straight down into the depths of the channel.

"Hot damn! Now we're talkin'!"

Drake steadied the boat while Bob reeled in his line to get it out of Jerome's way. Aria got the net and handed it to Bob.

Sensitive to the moods of the ocean, Aria felt the current battling the ebbing tide. The tug-of-war vibrated through the hull.

"Don't let that sucker get away," Bob said.

"Keep the line taut," Drake reminded the fisherman.

Jerome cranked the handle on the reel; sweat beaded his forehead; muscles weakened by too much sitting at a desk pulled hard and corded his arms.

The mild anxiety that had been nagging at Aria turned into full-blown fear. She'd had no idea until now how powerfully the tide shifted in these waters. Drake's warning had understated the danger. "We've got to go," she urged.

"Relax. I know these waters like the back of my hand, and I know just how hard I can push my boat. We'll be okay if Jerome can haul that baby in within a couple of minutes," he insisted.

"It's not worth the risk."

She could see in Drake's eyes he thought it was. She sensed he was courting the fine edge of disaster to prove he was a better fishing guide than Chuck Lampert. Such foolish pride, however friendly the rivalry. None of it was necessary. It was, however, typical male behavior, she realized—both mermen and human males apparently suffered from the same overdose of ego. In some respects, such a weakness was actually endearing.

But now it could be dangerous.

The fish broke the surface of the water, leaping into the air off the stern of the boat in a desperate effort to escape.

Jerome whooped a vulgar cheer. "Come to Papa, baby."

The flow of the tide accelerated.

"Drake, we're running out of time." From the corner of her eye, Aria caught the flash of another tail waving above the water's surface. She glanced quickly in that direction to identify the species but it had already dived out of sight, leaving Aria with the troubling afterimage of a silver flukes that looked suspiciously as if they could belong to a mermaid.

For once she hoped she was wrong and that no other mermaid was passing through these waters, especially not her wicked stepmother.

Leaning over the railing, Bob maneuvered the net as Jerome brought his fish closer.

"I've got it!" Bob shouted.

"Hang on, gentlemen. We're getting out of here." Giving the boat full throttle, Drake wheeled them around and headed them south, away from the narrows as Bob dropped the fish-filled net onto the deck. For an instant, it felt as though the tide wasn't going to let them go. The engine strained; the boat seemed anchored to some powerful force. Then the boat surged forward toward safe water.

Exhaling the breath she'd been holding, Aria's legs gave way and she sank onto the box where gear was stored on deck. Meanwhile, the men were congratulating each other. She suspected none of the three of them—not even Drake—realized just how close they had come to disaster. After all, a mermaid had far more knowledge of traveling through treacherous waters than any human male could possibly possess. And, as a rule, they were likely to have considerably more good sense.

"Promised you we'd have great fishing," Drake bragged to the two fishermen. He winked at Aria.

Her heart did a little stutter step and she shook her head. Perhaps all human males were slightly crazy when it came to fishing and that's why they were so easily lured to their deaths by a wily mermaid.

Smiling broadly, Jerome held up the bass at the end of his line. It was a good three feet long, and thick around the middle. "This baby might not be a record, but it's a damn good catch. Well done, Hart."

They sped through the widening strait toward a boat that hadn't ventured quite so far into the narrows. Drake shouted over the roar of the engines, "Hold up your catch, gentlemen. The albacore, too. Let those poor misguided suckers see 'em and weep."

With glee, Jerome and Bob complied with Drake's request. Aria noted the man at the helm of the other boat was Chuck Lampert. Smugly, Drake

waved to his friend and Chuck tipped his hat in response. Aria could almost see an I'll-get-you-next-
time promise in his eyes, and she laughed in spite
of herself at their determined rivalry.

ADRENALINE was still surging through Drake's
veins even after he had let his clients off at Sechelt
and returned to Hart's Cove. Damn, he felt good!

With the waning afternoon, the winter white sun
had dipped below the horizon, streaking a few scattered clouds with a trace of pink, and the temperature had dropped to a bracing forty degrees.

After securing the boat to the dock, he dropped
down into the cabin where Aria was cleaning up the
galley. She'd taken off her jacket and had rolled up
the sleeves of her sweatshirt while she washed a few
dishes in the sink.

"I owe you, Aria."

She turned and looked up at him with eyes that
looked almost jade in the subdued light. Her cheeks
were flushed a light rose from a day in the sun and
wind. "Owe me?"

"I don't know how you did it, but I doubt I ever
could have located all those fish today. You were
incredible."

"You took a great risk in the narrows." A slight
movement of the boat caused her to sway toward
him.

Instinctively he placed his hands on her shoulders
to steady her. "I had everything under control." His
control was slipping now, however. The slope of her

shoulders was too thoroughly feminine, her shapely figure too inviting.

"You knew how dangerous the narrows could be, yet you lingered there simply to catch one more fish."

He studied her lips, the lower one slightly fuller that the top. The adrenaline in his system pumped up a notch. What he wanted to do now was a hell of a lot more risky than running against a tidal surge.

"Aria, I need to know." He swallowed hard. "Are you married?"

With a puzzled frown, she shook her head.

"Are you sure there's no man in Nanaimo looking for you?"

"Positive."

He wanted to believe her; he *had* to believe her because he couldn't *not* kiss her, and maybe do a whole lot more if she was willing.

Tentatively, Aria moved a little closer and rested her palms on his chest. His heart beat fast and hard. So did hers. Only a narrow circle of dark brown surrounded the black iris of his eyes. Though she didn't understand the details, she sensed the moment was near. Soon Drake would share his milt with her. The surge of pleasure that went through her, tingling her breasts and creating a strange, heated sensation somewhere low in her midsection, surprised her. She could imagine no other male with whom she would want this to happen.

As he lowered his head, she lifted her lips to meet

his. A kiss was the beginning, she realized, but only the first step in a process she was eager to learn.

She'd never felt anything so soft yet firm, never tasted anything so sweet and succulent as Drake's lips and tongue. She savored his flavor. His masculine scent surrounded her, penetrating her senses as thoroughly as his tongue delighted her mouth. An exciting warmth swept through her, hot enough to ward off the deepest winter chill.

His hands skimmed across her back and pulled her hips against the hard ridge of his body. Excitement sped through her like a tidal wave.

"Ah, Aria, you're so damn sexy." His voice was low and gravelly, inviting an intimacy that she, too, demanded.

She had to get closer. Much closer. "Take off your jacket," she whispered, her throat so tight with anticipation she was surprised she could speak at all. "And your shirt."

"You sure, Aria? 'Cause if you're not—" He gave a low growl when her palms first made contact with his bare chest.

She traced the intriguing pattern of hair she found, fascinated by the slight roughness and the warp of warm, pliable flesh stretched over hard, masculine muscles. Her heartbeat accelerated at the thought of what else she might discover. A nipple pebbled beneath her fingertips. Two of them.

Drake groaned. "Oh, baby…"

She smiled and licked first one nipple and then

the other. The salty flavor reminded her of the sea. Of coming home.

With a deftness that startled her, Drake pulled her sweatshirt off over her head, then returned the favor by suckling her nipples as she had laved his. In some magical way, the cabin began to spin as if they were caught in a whirlpool.

Suddenly Aria's legs were as useless to her as a mermaid's tail on land, unable to hold her upright. They'd lost all of their strength. But it didn't matter. Drake effortlessly carried her to the narrow bunk and laid her on the soft mattress. She hadn't realized the strength of a fisherman, the corded brawn of his arms, the muscular power of his thighs, revealed when he removed his pants.

Her eyes widened and she gasped at the sight of his arousal nesting in a dark thatch of hair. A human male was quite a fascinating creature, though it was troubling to speculate just how and where he might use that impressive appendage.

Before she could conjure any clear image, he was kissing her again, stroking her in intimate places, and nothing else mattered. She'd had no idea her legs would be so sensitive to his touch, especially there at the back of her knees. Or there, she sighed, when his lips brushed against her inner thigh.

His fingers slid between her legs. She bucked against his hand and called his name.

"It's okay, sweetheart. It's okay."

"Yes. Oh, yes." She was drowning in a sea of sensation. It surged through her in curling waves of pleasure, washing over her and through her. Cleansing. As exhilarating as riding the crest of a tsunami.

Momentarily his weight lifted away from her, leaving her feeling as though she was treading water. She tried, and failed, to catch her breath. From a drawer beside the bed he pulled out a silver packet and ripped it open. Awash with wanting, she watched without understanding. She only knew there was more. Much more. And she wanted it all. Needed it all. Her life depended upon it.

He sank down next to her again and she welcomed him with open arms. He kissed her cheeks and lips and eyelids, each with a tender caress. His fingers threaded through her hair.

"You are, beyond a doubt, the most beautiful woman I have ever known." With that, he claimed her mouth again in a deep, probing kiss and spread her legs.

A flash of pain accompanied the moment he entered her with that fascinating appendage she'd noted earlier. Almost as quickly, the unpleasant sensation was gone, replaced by a tempest of swirling heat that remained and spread. She dug her fingers into his shoulders in the hope that she could hang on. But she spun out of control, her world going topsy-turvy as though she'd been caught in the curl of a somersaulting wave.

Giving a shout, Drake seemed to join her in that exhilarating moment, and they rode the crest together.

Slowly the world righted itself. She floated on a

buoyant sea, exquisitely aware of his weight, the dampness of his skin on hers and the rasp of his breathing. In a distant way, she was conscious of the sound of water lapping at the sides of the boat and the tug of the mooring lines as the sea gently rocked them.

Drake burrowed his face into the crook of Aria's neck. He hated the thought of moving—wasn't even sure he could. He felt drained as he had never felt before. She was such an incredibly sexy woman.

Thank God one of his prior clients, who'd enjoyed a leisurely afternoon below deck, had left a supply of condoms behind, or Drake would have been sweating tacks for fear he'd gotten Aria pregnant.

He didn't want to go through that scene again, no matter how good the woman made him feel.

Rising up on his elbows, he kissed her tenderly. A night floodlight that marked the end of the dock cast a faint glow through the cabin window. It occurred to him that it had been a very long time since he'd had a woman to share his victories with, or his defeats. "You okay?"

She smiled dreamily. "Oh, yes, I think so."

"Me, too. Never better, in fact." He kissed her again. "Maybe they're right about oysters."

Her eyes widened. "What oysters?"

"Never mind." He chuckled and forced himself to withdraw. "I hate to say it, but I think I'd better go pick up Matt. Alice Kelly will be wondering what happened to us."

"And Matt might be worried."

Rolling off the bunk, Drake searched for his discarded clothes on the floor. "You take your time getting up to the house, sweetheart. Alice said she'd send a ham home for supper tonight. They smoke 'em themselves."

She swung her legs over the side of the bunk totally unconcerned that she was as naked as the day she was born. He'd never known anyone so completely uninhibited, in or out of bed. Lips quirking, he figured he could learn to live with that.

"Drake, I don't know how to cook—"

"I'll take care of it. You won't even have to lift a finger—unless you want to open a can of veggies."

"That, I can manage," she said with a laugh that rippled through him like fine wine.

He tugged on his jeans and slipped his feet into his boots without bothering to tie the laces. As he shoved his arms into his shirt, he bent over to kiss her again. Damn, she tasted good! "I'll see you in a little while. Okay?"

"I'll be there."

Feeling like a million dollars, he went up on deck, hopped over the railing to the dock and strolled toward the house, whistling a tune from an old Elvis CD. He stopped at the house only long enough to get the keys to his Jeep and switch on the oven. He wanted the oven preheated when he brought the ham home, because he had some important plans for after dinner. Lingering over meal preparation would simply slow things down.

STRETCHING LANGUOROUSLY, Aria tried to ignore a niggling suspicion something wasn't quite right.

Certainly what she and Drake had just done had been more than pleasant. She'd learned, in several respects, the human anatomy had definite advantages over that of merpeople.

But in terms of sharing and accepting milt, something had gone wrong.

Sitting on the bed, she switched on a light. She pulled open the drawer beside the bunk and studied the small box she found. If only she could read, perhaps she would know what was inside.

"*T* is for a man with his arms sticking straight out, *R* is a humpbacked man with a cane, *O* is for—" She sighed.

It was useless. Even if she identified all the letters, she wouldn't know what they meant when they were put together.

Still curious, she ripped open one of the packets from the box. Drake had several remaining, so she didn't think he'd mind.

Trying to recall what she'd seen him do, she attempted to unroll the rubbery circle over her thumb. Apparently she lacked the proper technique. It lay there limply. Discouraged because she couldn't figure out what the thing was for, she twirled it around.

On a whim, she brought the elastic mouth to her lips and blew. Hard. The device expanded into the shape of a long, fat hot dog. She tied the open end in a knot and idly batted it in the air.

How odd.

Only a mermaid with exceptionally powerful lungs could possibly manage to inflate such a stiff balloon. And she was no closer than before to knowing why Drake felt it necessary to have a T-R-O-J-A-N handy when sharing his milt.

She'd have to ask him later. Strangely, she thought his answer might be important.

After dressing, she went up on deck. A light breeze had kicked up, carrying with it the scent of...

Smoke!

"SO HOW'D IT GO playing with Tommy?" After putting the ham from Alice in the back seat, Drake slid behind the wheel of the Jeep. Matt got in the passenger side.

"Mrs. Kelly made us t-take a nap."

"That bad, eh?" Drake laughed. It appeared he'd had a far better day than his son, particularly during the past hour or so, although the fishing had been memorable, too.

"Yeah, and Tommy kept saying he thought he was gonna upchuck, but he didn't tell his mom."

Drake frowned. "Why not?"

"I dunno. Besides, Tommy was being a j-jerk. He wouldn't even believe Aria's a m-mermaid."

"He wouldn't?" His lips canting into a smile, Drake recalled he had good reason not to believe that story, either. If he closed his eyes, he could still feel her shapely legs wrapped around his waist. No mermaid he'd ever heard about could do that.

"Maybe you shouldn't make up any more wild stories about mermaids, son."

Folding his arms, Matt scrunched down in his seat and pouted.

Drake was about to turn out of the Kelly driveway onto the island's dirt road, when he spotted the headlights of a vehicle approaching. It turned out to be Willy Wallace in his patrol car. Drake waited and Willy stopped.

"Hey, Hart, I was just on my way to your place." The policeman got out of his car and strolled across the road.

"Yeah? What's up?"

"I've got the photo of that missing woman from Nanaimo. Thought you'd like to take a look."

Drake swung out of the Jeep, his stomach knotting. In his whole life, he'd never messed with a married woman. He hoped to God he hadn't made a mistake this time.

Handing him a flyer with a black-and-white picture, Willy asked, "This the woman who showed up at your place?"

Relief eased the tension from Drake's tight shoulders as he studied the picture in the glare from the headlights. "No. That's not Aria. She's pretty, though." But not nearly as strikingly beautiful as Aria.

"Yeah, she's a looker. I hope she was on that ferry and is long gone. I'd hate to find her washed up on some beach around here."

"So would I."

Waving at Matt in the Jeep, Willy took back the flyer. "Guess that means you still don't know who the lady is who moved in with you."

"She isn't exactly living with me." Though that thought had considerable appeal at the moment. "She's staying in one of the cabins."

"Well, if you still want to ID her, all I can suggest is to get her prints. I'll run 'em through the system, if you want. As a favor, you understand. It's not exactly, ah, legal."

At the moment, Drake didn't much care who Aria was. But that was probably shortsighted. She might still be on the run from somewhere—or someone. "We'll see," he said noncommittally.

"Glad I caught you, anyway. Saves me a trip." He waved a casual salute and walked back to his car.

Drake returned to his vehicle, climbed in and shifted into gear. Though he was pleased Aria wasn't the missing woman, he still had a lot of unanswered questions about who she really was. He'd thought age and experience would make him immune to a pretty face, shapely legs and alluring green eyes. Or at least slow him down a little.

Not even close.

If resisting Aria had been some test to see if he'd learned anything in the past six years, he'd failed dismally.

Celibacy was hell on good sense.

During the ride home, Drake learned little about Matt's activities during the day, except that the boys had played Robocop in the Kelly tree house, and they'd driven off three or four sets of aliens.

Too much TV, he decided.

He pulled into his usual parking spot near the dock and glanced toward the house, anticipating a warm welcome from Aria.

"What the—"

He leaped out of the Jeep almost before it had come to a full stop and ran toward the house. Lights blazed. Every window was open, and rank-smelling, wispy smoke was pouring out of every damn one of them. Inside, a shadowy figure was frantically waving a towel in the air.

He yanked open the door to the house. Buffy, her fur standing straight out like a porcupine, ran between his legs in her frantic effort to escape, and nearly knocked him over in the process. "What the hell is going on?"

"Someone turned on the oven!" Red-faced, Aria brandished the towel like a bullfighter chasing a horde of marauding bulls.

"*I* turned it on."

"Sweet sea serpents! Why did you do that?"

"I wanted to preheat—"

"Didn't you think to look inside?"

"Of course not. Why would I—" He scowled. "What the hell was in there?"

She hooked her wrist on her hip. "Dirty dishes, that's what was in there. Everything's caked on the plates. They're all black and sticky. The milk's dried like bird droppings in the cereal bowls. Now I'll

never get them clean." She hiccupped and wiped
the back of her hand across her eyes, leaving a
streak of soot on her cheek. "You should have
looked!"

"You're supposed to *wash* dishes, not put 'em in
the oven."

"Oh, y-y-you," she wailed.

Matt came bouncing into the kitchen. "Wow,
does it ever stink in here. It's gross!"

"Yeah," Drake agreed grimly. "Somewhere I've
got a fan. Assuming I can find it, maybe we can
blow some of the smell out of here." He noted Aria
had gotten the dishes out of the oven and they were
piled helter-skelter on the counter, a singed tea towel
tossed on top of the heap. The caked-on spatter inside the oven looked terminal. It was going take a
jackhammer to get it all off.

Only a fair piece of luck had prevented Aria from
burning down the house.

He speared his fingers through his hair. "Ah,
hell!" Even Janie hadn't done anything this stupid.
If his home was going to survive intact, he would
have to hope Lillian would get back from her daughter's house soon.

It took two hours to clean up the kitchen and get
rid of the lingering smoke, if not quite all the odor.
They ate a cold ham dinner in silence; even Matt
was subdued by the heavy weight of hostility in the
room. That was fine with Aria. She had nothing to
say to Drake. He shouldn't have yelled at her. Mer-

maids weren't *supposed* to know anything about keeping house.

With great drama, *he* washed the dinner dishes, rolling up his sleeves and plowing his hands into the soapy water. If she'd still had a tail, she would have swiped him with it. Maybe even knocked him over.

"Time for bed, Matt," Drake announced. He wiped his hands on a dish towel.

"Aw, Dad..."

Drake's eyes narrowed. "This isn't a good time to argue with me, son."

Aria thought she should leave, too. Quickly. In fact, the cabin might not be far enough away to escape Drake's ire. But she hadn't had a chance to ask him what a T-R-O-J-A-N was, and her unsatisfied curiosity would very likely cause a sleepless night—and bring back certain intimate memories she didn't want to think about right now.

So she followed Matt down the hallway to his room. There was a big stuffed animal in the middle of his bed and colorful flags decorated the walls. From the amount of clutter on the floor, Aria concluded Matt wasn't particularly good at keeping his room clean, even if he had received a badge for his efforts. "Small-fry, if I told you the letters in a word, could you tell me what it means?"

"I guess so, if it's not too big a word."

Aria said each letter carefully, remembering the pictures they made in her mind. Matt wrote them down on a scrap of paper.

"I think that spells—" his forehead puckered "—Tro...jan."

She frowned. "What does that mean?"

His slender shoulders lifted in a shrug. "I dunno. It sounds kinda like a football team to me."

That made no sense in the context of what she and Drake had done that afternoon. "Why would your father have a box of Tro—"

A large, masculine hand closed around her upper arm and dragged her unceremoniously toward the hallway. "It's past your bedtime, son. I'll see you in the morning." He switched off the bedroom light and closed the door.

"What in the name of Neptune are you doing?" she sputtered.

He propelled her into the living room. In a low, threatening voice meant not to carry to the rest of the house, he said, "More to the point, why are you talking to my six-year-old son about condoms?"

She looked at him dumbly. "What are condoms?"

"Trojan condoms! Isn't that what you were asking him about?"

"Well, yes, but I wanted to know why you—"

"He's only six years old. How would he know?"

"Well, I don't know, either, and I'm a lot older than he is." She lifted her chin defiantly. "If you're so smart, why don't you tell me?"

Drake thought sure he was going to strangle this woman. She'd practically burned down his house. Now she was giving his son an early and unauthorized sex education lesson—and letting on as if she didn't know what she had done. Her multiple transgressions came pretty darn close to canceling out the spectacular fishing trip. And maybe even their spectacular lovemaking.

Particularly the lovemaking, he thought, recognizing that old-fashioned lust had gotten him into plenty of trouble before.

Using his most intimidating expression, he got in her face. So close he could see the sweep of her blond lashes and breathe the same air that she had just exhaled. Sweet and sexy. Tempting!

Damn! He wanted her again. Now! Even though he was mad as hell!

"I use condoms because I believe in responsible sex, unlike some women I've met. Most particularly, I used a condom today so I wouldn't get you pregnant. Now, will you stop asking my kid about Trojans?"

Aria blanched. "You don't want me to get pregnant?"

"Of course not." An irritating twitch developed in his right eye. "We hardly know each other. Besides, I told you I'm a confirmed bachelor. Hell, you ought to be thanking me for trying to be responsible about this whole thing."

Tears pooled in her eyes and her lower lip trembled. "Drake Hart, I don't think I like you very much." She whirled and stormed out of the house.

Fists clenched, Drake stood in the middle of the living room cursing himself. It was all he could do not to go after Aria. He hadn't handled the situation very well.

In fact, he'd just about blown it sky-high.

Why did women have to be such a damn mystery to men? He'd tried to do the right thing, and look where it had gotten him. He swore he would never figure out the opposite sex.

Besides, who the hell didn't know what a condom was?

If Aria was up to some game, he sure didn't know the rules.

ARIA MARCHED down the dock, climbed over the railing onto Drake's boat and went below deck.

She'd teach him a thing or two.

Not want to get her pregnant? Her life depended upon just that. And she wasn't going to let some pompous human male get in her way.

She jammed her fist against her mouth to stop her trembling chin. Darn it all, she wanted to have Drake's baby. Was that such a terrible crime? She wouldn't ask anything else of him. Just a bit of milt...

Yanking open the drawer, she picked up the box of condoms and glared down at the little silver packets.

Slowly, a plan came to her. She hadn't lived in shark-infested waters most of her life without picking up some of their wily ways. This appeared to be the time to employ just such cunning.

Fifteen minutes later she silently slipped off the boat and strolled up the walk past Drake's house to her cabin.

Chapter Eight

Aria sat bolt upright in bed.

In the lingering moments before dawn, a siren song drifted on the mist—ethereal and tempting. It was meant to lure an unwary sailor away from his night watch and send him to his death.

Oceana!

No other mermaid sang in the same otherworldly way. In this case Aria suspected Oceana wanted to entice not a sailor, but a fellow mermaid into showing herself. On the boat yesterday, she thought she had caught sight of the silver flash of a mermaid's tail. Now the one mermaid she'd never wanted to see again was calling to her.

Dressing hurriedly, she slipped out the cabin door and cast a longing glance down the bluff. Drake's house sat in the silent shadow of the hillside. She'd lain awake a good part of the night wishing he would come to her. Her body had pulsed with the need and the tactile memories of his caresses. But she'd heard no soft footsteps on the gravel path, no cautious knock on her door.

Willing herself to ignore the salty tears that had dampened her pillow, she had concentrated on coming up with a plan that would get her pregnant soon. No ready solution came to her. So in time she had fallen asleep.

Now, in search of Oceana, she took the rocky trail that led to the entrance of Hart's Cove. The ground was wet and slick, the uneven rocks slippery and the footing precarious. Around the point, the water kissed the shoreline in a determined whisper that promised to wear down any and all resistance.

With a matching sigh, Aria vowed that she'd do the same with Drake. It was imperative.

She lingered for a moment behind a fir at the tip of the point and observed her stepmother sitting on a low-lying rock, combing her long hair. The copious curls were the distinctive shade of blond common to most mermaids born in tropical waters. Oceana was not much older than Aria. Her features were classically beautiful, in contrast to a heart that was supremely cruel. Her silver tail swept lazily back and forth in the water as though moving to the rhythm of the sea.

The rising sun streaked the water with a rose-colored brush. So beautiful, Aria thought, resenting the way her stepmother's presence brought a sense of ugliness to the tranquil scene.

Restraining a surge of animosity, Aria stepped out of her hiding place. "Why have you come here?"

"Ah, there you are, my dear. A loving daughter come to greet her mother."

"*Step*mother," Aria corrected. Her mother had been the personification of goodness, a trait that appeared totally lacking in Oceana. With a heart that weighed heavily in her chest, Aria wondered again at how easily her father had been duped by an alluring voice and the meaningless mask of physical beauty.

"I see you were foolish enough to come out of the water during a full moon. Tsk, tsk. Your father would be quite disappointed in you."

"It was an accident. I—" She didn't have to defend her actions to Oceana. "You haven't answered my question. These waters are not suitable for a mermaid."

"So I have discovered." With a shiver, she pulled a heavy strand of hair through her fingers, combing out the knots. "I can't think why you chose this area. But then, in spite of all the bragging your father did, I often questioned your intelligence, my dear."

"Is that so?" Aria barely resisted the temptation to throw a rock or two in Oceana's direction—big ones that would knock her off her arrogant pedestal. "Then I'd say you are even more foolish than I to have followed me this far north. Yet here you are."

"The harbor seals lied to me. They said there were others like ourselves in these waters."

"They didn't lie. They were mistaken, mislead by lifeless statues that resemble mermaids."

Snorting an unladylike sound, Oceana ended the baiting game of shark and rockfish, and her expression turned malevolent. As the sun edged above the trees, it cast harsh shadows on her face. Ugliness replaced Oceana's superficial beauty, as though the sun had illuminated her soul. "Some of our people apparently held you in greater esteem than I had estimated. They were quite unhappy with me after you left."

Aria's eyes widened at the implication of her step mother's admission. "You mean you were banished from the village the same way you forced me to leave?" Ah, sweet justice! The sea gods are wise indeed.

"Don't look so smug, little Miss Uppity. I'll have my revenge before I'm through." Oceana slid off the rock into the water. With a thrust of her tail, she stroked closer to shore. "Did you enjoy your little fishing expedition yesterday?"

"You saw us?" A frisson of fear swept through Aria before she could repress it. Her stepmother, she knew, was capable of all sorts of evil deeds—she'd lured boats onto rocky shoals and caused men to leap over the side of their ships into the water and to their deaths. There was little Oceana wouldn't do if it struck her fancy.

"I saw you and your handsome boat captain, my dear. He seemed quite taken with you."

"You're wrong." Sensing danger, Aria was quick to deny Drake had any interest in her. Which, given his unwillingness to share his milt, was all too close to the truth. "He has hired me only to do his house-keeping." And had found her skills lacking.

"Then you won't mind if I toy with the man a bit. His actions appeared reckless enough yesterday that he should be easy prey—"

"Leave Drake alone. He's done you no harm."

"Ah, but *you* have, my sweet, darling daughter. First you spoke against me to your father."

"I did no such thing. He saw for himself how wicked you were, but by then it was too late. You had already snared him into your seductive trap." A large measure of guilt still rode on Aria's shoulders because she hadn't acted to protect her father from making a foolish mistake—the bonding to a mermaid who didn't deserve to share his kingdom.

Continuing her litany of grievances against Aria, Oceana said, "Then, because of you, the villagers turned against me."

"You drove me away. How is what happened after I left *my* fault?"

"Because I say so. And do not think for a moment I will not retaliate against those who have done me harm. I would have been a revered queen of the merpeople were it not for you." She angrily swiped with her tail at an innocent gull that had settled peacefully in the water nearby. Cawing a noisy objection, the bird took flight. "It would be sweet, indeed, if I could destroy this boat captain of yours before he managed to assure your final transformation into a human. And then, when you return to the sea, I shall destroy you as well."

Aria felt the blood drain from her face, her fear not for herself, but for the man who had rescued her when she had floundered. "I won't let you hurt Drake."

Oceana's beautifully sculpted features twisted into a grotesque mask of hatred. "You cannot stop me. Or perhaps it would be better yet if I simply tell your captain that you are a mermaid. We both know how a human male would react to that news." With that final threat and a sharp, bitter laugh, she dived out of sight beneath the water.

Simultaneously a boat appeared at the mouth of Hart's Cove, the sun glinting off the brass railings.

The breath in Aria's lungs snagged on a lump of fear. Drake and Matt were going somewhere. Through no fault of their own, they might well be in mortal danger.

Before Aria could shout a warning, Drake accelerated, revving the engine to full speed, leaving the faint circle of Oceana's wave in his wake, easily outrunning any mermaid who might follow.

Aria gave profound thanks to the sea gods for their intervention. Both Drake and her secret were safe for the moment.

As soon as Drake reached Oyster Bay, he went to Willy's office, arriving as the policeman was opening up for the day. He followed him inside and placed a brown paper bag on the desk.

"What's that?" Willy asked. He tossed the office keys next to the bag.

Glancing over his shoulder, Drake made sure Matt was still engaged in watching a commercial fishing boat preparing to cast off. "It's a glass. Aria drank out of it last night." Drinking water she'd liberally salted, an idiosyncrasy that she had demonstrated more than once, to Drake's amusement. "I was careful not to touch the outside of the glass and made sure it didn't get washed. I thought—"

"You want me to run the prints?"

"Yeah, I do." He shoved the bag across the desk toward Willy, then jammed his hands in his jacket pockets. He needed to know who Aria really was before getting involved any deeper—as if that were possible. He was already thinking about her every waking moment, and even while he slept, Aria had an uncanny ability to find her way into his dreams.

"It'll take a while to get the results back."

He forced a noncommittal shrug. "No hurry." Tomorrow would be just barely soon enough to have the answers he wanted. This afternoon would even top that. But he'd have to live with the snail's pace of government bureaucracy. "Let me know when you hear anything."

Turning, he strolled unhurriedly to the door and let himself out. He felt like a scuzz ball. He shouldn't have yelled at Aria. If she was hiding out from someone, that was her business and he should leave it alone. Except he couldn't.

She was driving him crazy.

If he didn't get himself under control, he was going to need a whole case of T-R-O-J-A-N-S.

He swore under his breath! Now she even had him spelling his thoughts!

ARIA KNEW the instant Drake became aware of her approach. She could see it in the sudden tautness of his body, in the grim tightness around his beautiful mouth. The hammer stilled in his hand, the repairs to the padded canvas bumper around a boat slip temporarily halted. But he didn't look at her. He simply knelt there on the dock, waiting in the quiet of late morning.

Waiting for what? she wondered.

She swallowed hard. How could she protect him from Oceana if he wouldn't even talk to her?

After her stepmother's threats, Aria had considered leaving Hart's Cove. If that sacrifice would mean Drake and his son would be safe, she would have gone. Truly, she would have. But once Oceana had made up her vindictive mind that someone was her enemy, she was like a shark in a feeding frenzy. No matter what the truth might be, she never changed her mind.

By helping Aria, Drake had made it to the top of Oceana's list of foes to be destroyed, right up there with Aria herself.

Oceana had also made it all the more impossible for Aria to return to her life as a mermaid, even if she were to safely reach warmer waters. Oceana would pursue her to the ends of the seas to get her revenge.

Legs, and the ability to run far and fast on dry land, were Aria's best defenses. Pregnancy had become even more imperative in order to retain her new appendages—and her life.

Taking a deep breath, she swallowed her pride and issued a quiet apology to Drake. "I'm sorry about the dishes in the oven."

His tight grip on the hammer eased and his shoulders relaxed. "I shouldn't have yelled at you."

"No, that wasn't very nice of you."

"Look, Aria..." He stood and gazed down at her, his expressive brows leveled into a troubled line. "I think we got carried away yesterday. You know, the excitement of a successful fishing trip. The adrenaline can start pumping, and a man can go kind of crazy."

She swayed forward. Intentionally. Purposefully. Her goal was to protect both herself and Drake from a threat he certainly wouldn't understand and would probably deny existed. The only way she could do that was to cast her own spell over him, one so powerful Oceana would never be able to lure him to his death with her bittersweet songs. "Are you sorry you mated with me?"

The muscles in his throat corded and moved convulsively. "*Mated?* You sure have a crazy way of putting things, but no, I'm not sorry. It was terrific."

"How nice of you to say so." Aria chafed at such small praise, when she'd thought it the most glorious experience ever. "Then perhaps we should repeat the process?"

"That's not a good plan, Aria."

"Are you promised to some other woman?"

"Me? No. It's just that..." Jamming the hammer into his tool belt, Drake searched for a way to explain his feelings. It wasn't that he was insensitive to a woman's vulnerabilities after she'd made love. He understood that and felt a little exposed himself. In fact, in some bizarre way, Aria seemed more defenseless than most women he'd known, even though she was amazingly open about having a sexual relationship. Maybe that was what scared him to death. He kept slipping out of control, and she didn't lift a finger or mutter a single word to keep him in check.

A woman was supposed to resist a man's advances for a little while, wasn't she? Whatever happened to playing hard to get?

Unless she didn't care who she slept with.

He didn't want to think that of Aria. But he hadn't wanted to classify Janie as promiscuous, either. Until it had been rubbed in his face.

Damn, there was no way he could trust his own judgment, not based on his track record. He'd sworn he'd spend at least six months getting to know a woman before he made a commitment again. With Aria it hadn't even been two weeks.

The drone of an airplane engine caused Drake to look up. A yellow and white Cessna circled overhead, wobbled its wings, then turned into the light breeze to land just outside the cove.

"My gracious, who's that?" Aria asked. Using her hand, she shaded her eyes from the glare of the midday sun.

"Chuck Lampert."

"Your friend? How nice."

Drake figured *nice* wasn't on his buddy's agenda. He'd probably flown over here to impress Aria. From the looks of her eager smile, he'd done just that.

"Hey, D-Dad," Matt yelled as he came running toward the end of the dock. "It's Chuck."

"Yeah, I know."

The float plane taxied up to the dock, and Chuck cut the engine. A moment later the door opened.

"How's it going, Hart? Aria?" In a friendly salute, he touched his fingertips to the brim of his baseball cap. "You too, squirt."

Matt bounded back and forth on the dock checking out the plane. "Man, I wish we had a p-plane."

"What are you doing here, Lampert?" Drake asked.

"Thought I'd give you a fighting chance to get even."

Drake's forehead tightened. "Even at what?"

"Yesterday, while you were risking your neck and your charter in the narrows, I spotted a humongous white sea bass. Based on the flukes, I'd guess she was close to five feet."

Aria gasped. It was easy to assume Chuck had spotted the same tail she had seen—Oceana's.

"Five feet? That would be a record for these waters." Drake eyed Chuck suspiciously. Friend or not, a true sportsman didn't give away that kind of information for free. "So why are you telling me, instead of going after that fish yourself?"

Aria tried to jump into the conversation with an objection, but both men ignored her.

"Because you've been grousing for five years that I stole that trophy bass right off your line. Here's your chance to beat me out by landing a bigger one."

"I don't need your charity, Lampert. I can find my own trophies."

"This one has probably moved on, anyway," Aria added hopefully.

"Nope. A guy who went out this morning from Oyster Bay thought he'd seen the same fish down around the lighthouse feeding on a natural oyster bed."

Gritting her teeth, Aria wished Oceana would stay out of sight and take her meals far from Oyster Island. "That was probably someone who'd heard James's crazy stories about the Salmon Woman. I was down there the other day, and I certainly didn't see any big fish." She'd missed seeing Oceana that day, but had certainly come in contact with her since then.

"How do I know this isn't some prank you and Dudley have cooked up to send me out on a wild-goose chase?" Drake asked.

Goose chase? Aria rolled her eyes. What in the world did geese have to do with sea bass or vengeful mermaids?

"Do what you want. There's a bass out there for the taking. Meanwhile, I thought I'd take Aria over to Nanaimo for that sushi I promised her."

"Now I see what you're up to," Drake said in an accusatory tone. "You're trying to distract me with some fish story so you can have Aria all to yourself."

A guilty grin crossed Chuck's face. "I thought it might work. Besides, I did see that fish. Bet I tempted you, didn't I?"

"Might have," Drake conceded.

Aria leaped on the first idea that came to mind to prevent Drake from going after Oceana. "Let's all go to Nanaimo."

Matt cheered. "Yeah, me, too!"

"Some of us have work to do," Drake groused.

"No problem. I'll take Aria and the boy."

Drake unbuckled his tool belt and dropped it to the dock. No way was he going to trust Lampert with Aria, even if his son was along to chaperon. His work—and the sea bass Chuck had told him about—would have to wait.

"What are you waiting for, Lampert?" he challenged. "Let's get this show on the road."

SQUEEZING HER EYES tightly shut, Aria questioned the wisdom of anyone flying in a airplane. Surely if humans were intended to have wings, they would have been born with them. Just as she had been born with the necessary equipment to make her a superior swimmer. To trust one's life to these artificial wings was beyond foolhardy. She was terrified. Only the thought that she had kept Drake safe from Oceana prevented her from begging to be returned to Hart's Cove immediately.

And only the familiar taste of bite-size pieces of fresh tuna dipped in an intriguing sushi sauce revived her. She licked her fingers.

"You really like that stuff, don't you?" Chuck said. Drake had taken his son to the men's room and they were sitting alone at a window table that overlooked a huge harbor filled with boats and float planes.

"Hmm, delicious."

"We sure couldn't convince Matt to try it. All he wanted was a hamburger."

"For me, this sushi made it *almost* worth the flight. Thank you."

He laughed. "I gather you haven't ever flown in a small plane before."

"You gather correctly." Nor would she again, if there were any other way to get back to Hart's Cove. Riding in Drake's boat provided all the speed she could handle, and elevation, too.

Thoughtfully Chuck toyed with the straw in his soft drink. While Drake was dark and ruggedly handsome, Chuck was the opposite, fair and almost boyish in his appearance. "You and Drake seem to be getting along pretty good together."

"He's been very kind to me," she responded cautiously, wondering what Chuck had on his mind.

"When we were in school, Drake was the life of the party. We had a lot of fun together, and he was the best friend a guy could have. Then he got married.''

Made nervous by the intensity of his blue-eyed gaze, Aria sprinkled salt in her drinking water and sipped from the glass.

"Janie wasn't good for him," Chuck continued, his gaze straying to her glass and the salt shaker in her hand. "And she hurt him real bad by running around with other guys. It changed him. If it hadn't been for Matt, I don't know what he would have done. I'd hate for him to get hooked up with another woman like that.''

"So would I," she assured him. Recalling the intimacies they had shared on the boat together, she was unable to imagine why any woman would seek out another man if Drake was her mate.

Chuck studied her a moment, then grinned. "I'm real sorry he found you first, Aria. Real sorry.''

She felt a rush of heat flush her cheeks. Drake was indeed fortunate to have a friend like Chuck. She hoped he'd be her friend, too.

THE FLIGHT BACK to the island was slightly less terrifying than the first and mercifully short. Nonetheless, Aria was grateful when she could finally plant her feet solidly on the dock once again. Chuck waved goodbye from the cockpit, taxied out of the cove and took off into the lowering sun.

Tired of being cooped up, Matt ran toward the houseboat.

Drake sauntered over to pick up the tool belt he'd

dropped earlier. "There's enough daylight left, I think I'll go looking for the that sea bass Chuck spotted. Maybe down by the lighthouse."

Aria gasped. She thought he'd forgotten about that. "No, please! Don't go." She snared his arm, her fingers digging into rock-hard biceps.

He stared down at her hand. "What's wrong with you, Aria? I'm a fisherman. That's how I make my living and that's what I'm gonna do now—go fishing. I want it to be *my* fish mounted on Dudley's wall. Chuck's had the glory too long."

Panic and fear knotted in Aria's stomach. He was so committed to catching a giant sea bass, she'd never be able to convince Drake that Chuck had been wrong. The fluked tail he'd seen belonged to Oceana, not an ordinary fish. Unless she told the truth about the danger her stepmother posed, Drake would unknowingly put himself at terrible risk. And the only way to persuade him of the truth would be to admit that she, too, was a mermaid.

"You can handle Matt on your own, can't you?"

"Drake..." She swallowed hard. "There's something you should know."

"Da-ad!" Matt called from the house, his voice quivery and fearful. "I think you ought to c-come quick!"

For an instant, Aria met Drake's gaze. Then they both raced to see what was wrong with Matt.

IT WAS LATE EVENING before Matt was able to hold even a little broth in his stomach. Aria's heart went out to him, he'd been so miserable the past few hours. The only saving grace with the child's sudden illness had been that Drake couldn't go chasing after the elusive white sea bass he so coveted and, therefore, had remained safe from Oceana's treacherous allure for at least one more day. Instead, he'd made a quick trip to the mainland for medicine.

Sitting on the side of Matt's bed, she wiped a damp cloth across his forehead. "You go to sleep now, small-fry. The medicine your father gave you will make you feel much better by morning."

"I wish you could read me a story." Matt looked up at her with pleading, red-rimmed eyes. His cheeks were flushed with fever.

She pursed her lips. She could ask Drake to read to his son, but he'd spent most of the evening traveling to and from the mainland. With the wind picking up, she knew the return trip had been difficult, and she wanted him to have a chance to rest and eat a decent, albeit late, dinner before resuming his parental duties.

"I might not be able to read," she told Matt, "but I could tell you a story. Would you like that?"

"I guess so."

"Let me see..." Aria thought for a moment, trying to remember a suitable tale from the stories her people had told in the quiet of beautiful grottos.

"Once upon a time, a very long time ago in a far off kingdom beneath the sea, there lived a young prince named Frolic. He was a very happy little boy except for one thing."

"What was that?"

"There were no colors in Prince Frolic's kingdom. Wherever he swam, all he could see were shades of gray. The whales were a very dark gray, the eels were a medium gray and the fish were all light gray. It was very boring beneath the sea."

"That's how it is here sometimes in the winter. The clouds are gray all the time, and I get bored."

"Well, when Prince Frolic got very, very bored, like little boys sometimes do, he'd swim up to the top of the ocean. And there he'd see beautiful colors—green trees and blue skies and red and yellow flowers. He liked that very much."

Matt's eyelids were growing heavier by the moment, and they drooped closed.

Aria continued with her story, letting her voice soothe him. "So Prince Frolic went to his father, King Neptune, and he said, 'Why can't our kingdom be as beautiful as it is above the water?'

"Now the king was a very loving, understanding father—just like your father—and he decided his son was right. Their kingdom should be as colorful as any other kingdom on earth.

"And do you know what King Neptune did?"

Matt shook his head, but he was so close to sleep, he couldn't quite manage to open his eyes. Smiling, Aria caressed his flushed cheek with the back of her fingers.

"The king issued an edict to all of his subjects. The fish were to paint themselves with bright designs that would flash in the water when they swam.

And the crabs and shrimp were told to eat just the right foods so their shells would turn shades of red and pink. The king even told the coral it had to change. It could no longer be a dreary old boring gray. It had to pick something very colorful, and so the coral picked the brightest, most colorful shades of rose and red it could find.''

Noting Matt's steady breathing, she leaned over and brushed a kiss against his damp forehead before she ended the story.

''And since that very day until now, Prince Frolic has been happy to swim all morning and all afternoon in his beautiful, colorful sea. Then, at night, when he curls up in a very special place to sleep, he dreams his dreams in bright, vivid color. And that's why, in the warm tropical waters to the south, every fish is a true masterpiece of color, and Prince Frolic is such a happy little boy.''

Matt's little chest moved up and down in the rhythm of sleep, and Aria wished, in some deep spot near her heart that she hadn't known existed, that someday she would be gifted with a child as beautiful as this little boy.

Behind her, she heard a movement. Turning, she discovered Drake was standing in the doorway. There were lines of stress around his eyes, and tension bracketed his sensual mouth. In that instant she realized having a child involved far more than simply becoming pregnant.

Chapter Nine

Drake stepped into the room, aroused as much by Aria's tenderness as by his desire for her. In the circle of light from the bed lamp, she looked golden, her hair spilling in a guileless fall over her shoulder.

Somehow with Aria he'd jumped the gun, letting his lust get in the way of learning who she was as a woman. He'd repeated an old pattern, his only excuse being too many years of celibacy.

Now he suddenly wanted to start over and take the time they needed so he could trust his own judgment.

"My mother used to tell me stories," he said. He extended his hand, and her delicate fingers vanished into his much larger palm. When she stood, he led her to the living room where they could talk without disturbing Matt's much-needed rest. "I loved hearing all the old Indian legends about wily foxes, but my favorite was about a playful mink that was always getting into trouble. These days, with so much television, there aren't many storytellers left."

"I learned from my mother, too. Except that

particular tale was originally about a *Princess* Frolic—not a prince—who was forever getting bored."

He felt the hint of a smile curl his lips. "Why do I suspect she was talking about you?" Reluctantly he released her hand, and she sat down at the end of the couch, leaning her head back with a sigh that exposed the creamy column of her neck. Buffy hopped up into her lap and began to lick her fingers.

"That's very perceptive of you." Her light laughter was as delicate as ice crystals tinkling in the cold air, and her fingers stroked Buffy in a gentle caress that Drake found he envied. "I'm afraid I was a difficult child and far too impetuous for my mother's liking. She swore nothing good would come of me."

"She was wrong." Emotion tightened a knot in Drake's throat, not lust this time but something far more powerful, an emotion he was afraid to name. He worried that a place like Hart's Cove could never satisfy someone who'd been easily bored as a child. "You've become a beautiful, caring woman."

She smiled faintly. "It's true my mother would not have predicted that particular future for me."

"So tell me." He sat down on the opposite arm of the couch. "What did you do as a little girl when you got bored?"

Petting the cat, she pondered the question for a moment as though her childhood had been hundreds of years ago, or in a place so far away she could barely remember it. "Oh, I used to build sand castles on the beach with the other mer—" Her voice caught and she tried again. "With the other children. Or we'd have races to see who could swim the farthest or fastest."

"Did you win?" Given her lithe body, he suspected that was the case.

"Often, except when the older boys decided to play. They were always the fastest swimmers, but I could outlast them in a long race."

"I grew up playing soccer. Chuck and I were forwards on our high school team. We'd played together for so long, we could pass the ball to the other guy without even looking to see where he was."

"Teamwork."

"Yeah. It used to drive the opposition crazy." Those were good days, Drake recalled. Not many worries then, but responsibilities were right around the corner—taking over his father's business, failing at marriage and raising a son on his own.

"I sensed at Matt's Tiger Cub ceremony that you are a natural leader among the people of the village."

He shrugged off the compliment. "I wouldn't say that. They're all good, decent people who are trying to earn an honest living."

"I think you do not appreciate how much others respect you."

No, he guessed he hadn't given that much thought. Most of the time he was simply trying to take it one day at a time. But he liked that Aria thought he was worthwhile.

The air in the room became heavy, as though

they'd each become more aware of the other. The temptation to give up all semblance of restraint fought with Drake's new resolve to think of Aria as a whole woman, not just a female who stirred up his juices by simply looking at him. Which she was doing now.

As if responding to the awkward silence that fell between them, Aria's expression became pensive. She glanced toward the back of his house where his son slept. "The medicine you brought home seems to be helping Matt."

"Thank goodness." He was incredibly grateful she had found a neutral topic before he made a fool of himself. Again. "The poor kid was miserable."

"You were wonderful with him. So patient."

"Sometimes that's what a dad has to do." Though he suspected in most families the mother handled sick children. He noted with considerable approval that Aria had been a big help during the worst moments—even cleaning up some terrible messes his son had made—and Drake had trusted her completely to care for Matt while he went to the nearest pharmacy on the mainland. No man, or child, would have expected more of a natural mother.

"I called Alice Kelly after I got back from the mainland. She says Tommy is beginning to feel better already, so whatever bug Matt has, it wasn't the hamburger he ate and it probably won't last long."

He hunkered down to pick up a few toy cars and trucks that his son had left scattered around the room. "By tomorrow, or maybe the day after, I should be able to go after that trophy sea bass—assuming somebody else hasn't already landed it."

"I wish you wouldn't."

He lifted his gaze to meet hers and found a pair of troubled eyes looking back at him. "Why not?"

"Because it may not be a fish at all."

"What else could it be? A man-eating whale? Or some secret underwater weapon conjured up by the Royal Navy?"

Lowering her head, she laced her fingers together in her lap and studied them as though the answer to his question was woven through the graceful linkages. "It could be a mermaid."

The bizarre suggestion jarred him, however softly spoken it had been. She must have slipped back into her storytelling mode. That had to be why she'd said such a crazy thing.

"I suppose next you're going to tell me there are leprechauns in the woods, trolls under every bridge and the Martians have landed." He jammed his fingers through his hair. "It's one thing to make up stories for Matt, but I wish you'd trust me, Aria. I really do. Whatever secret you're trying to hide, it won't matter to me. I just don't want to hear any more nonsense from either you or Matt about mermaids. They don't exist and never have, any more than wily foxes or humorous minks."

With a wrenching sense of betrayal, he realized his mother had told him all those stories. And after she'd died, he'd been forced to grow up on his own only to discover that none of her stories had been true. There were no happy endings. He didn't want Matt to experience the same sense of disillusionment.

He levered himself to his feet. "Come on. You need your rest as much as Matt, if you don't want to come down with the flu bug. I'll walk you back to your cabin."

"It's not that far. Besides, I've been coming and going on my own since almost the first night I stayed there." As she stood, the cat tumbled out of her lap with a loud complaint.

"Well, this time I'm going to be a gentleman and walk you home." And that was all he was going to do, he promised himself, as he took a quick peek in Matt's room to be sure that his son was sleeping comfortably. He wasn't going to go inside Aria's cabin with her, or even sneak a good-night kiss on the porch. This time he was damn well going to be a gentleman, even if it killed him.

But as they walked up the path, his hand automatically sought hers, their fingers lacing together. And then, when the wind snared a strand of her hair, he instinctively brushed it back from her face. As his fingers brushed against her cheek, he sensed a responding shudder pass through Aria, one that suggested she would welcome more than a gentlemanly good-night.

Damn, being honorable was hell on a man's libido!

"How many more days until the moon is full?" she asked.

"I don't know." He followed her gaze toward the sliver of moon rising above the treetops. "Probably ten days or so."

"That isn't very long, is it?"

"I suppose that depends on what happens during those ten days, or what you think is going to happen when the moon is full."

"Under some circumstances, ten days would seem far too short a time."

He wasn't quite sure what to make of her comment, or her wistful sigh, so he let it slide.

Reaching the cabin, she stopped at the bottom step and looked up at him. In spite of the darkness, he detected an invitation in her eyes. Every cell in his body screamed for him to accept whatever she was willing to give. With a few quick strides, he'd be inside the cabin and she'd be there with him. They'd discard their clothes, and together they'd find paradise, a special fulfillment he'd rarely achieved.

Blood pulsed hot and heavy through his veins.

"Would you like to come in?" she asked.

"Yes." His voice strangled on his acceptance; his conscience gave him a quick kick in the butt. "No, I can't. Matt's alone. I shouldn't—"

"I understand." Her hand slipped away from his. "Perhaps in a few days when he's feeling better."

"Yeah, that would be fine." Nobility could certainly make a liar out of any man!

Turning, Aria went up the few remaining steps to the porch and let herself into the cabin. Frustration and failure weighed heavily on her shoulders.

She'd tried.

What more could a mermaid do?

Drake wouldn't share his milt with her, and she realized now that producing a child was something he didn't take lightly. His fatherly instincts were too well honed. In other things he might take unnecessary risks—like challenging the swiftly changing tides—but in this he was cautious.

And his refusal, however much it might be justified, could cost Aria her life.

Worse, she still didn't know how to protect Drake from his own weakness—his compulsive need to catch the biggest white sea bass on the planet and outshine Chuck Lampert in their friendly rivalry. His determination would put him squarely in the path of danger from Oceana's vendetta.

Moreover, the stubborn man didn't believe in mermaids. Instead, the look in his eye when she'd mentioned the topic suggested he thought she was a little crazy. So her warnings would go unheeded.

The dilemma spun through her head like tangled seaweed, and she spent a restless night searching for answers. Regret slid through her as sharp and cutting as coral when she realized her only choice might be to find another human male who would do the necessary deed in Drake's place.

DRAKE'S FEET hit the floor the next morning an instant after he heard the back door slam. A chorus of childish giggles was followed by a good deal of adult shushing. Lillian's stern admonitions were a wake-up call that reminded him all too clearly of his youth.

Groggy from lack of sleep, he pulled on his jeans and stumbled out into the kitchen. Four of Lil's grandkids were seated around his breakfast table—Toby, Peter, Joshua and Megan. The two-and-a-half-year-old had her thumb in her mouth.

"What's going on?" he asked, swiping his hand across his face in the useless hope that all these small creatures would vanish like a bad dream.

"My son-in-law got in the way of the saw at the mill," Lillian explained as she poured four bowls of cereal. "My daughter insists she's going to Vancouver where they took him for surgery. I can't let her go alone, not with her pregnancy so iffy, and her kids will be better off here with you than hanging around some hospital. Marcia and me are taking the eight-o'clock ferry."

Drake came wide awake. "You're leaving the kids with me?"

"You've got enough space if they double up some. Won't be for but two or three days, at the most. I've brought clothes for 'em and a couple of sleeping bags."

His gaze darted to the heap of belongings that had been dropped haphazardly beside the door. "But I can't—"

"You don't have any charters scheduled, do you?"

"Well, no, but—"

"Then you'll manage. Aria is still here, isn't she?"

"Sure, but…Lil, Matt came down with the stomach flu yesterday."

That brought Lillian's steamroller to a momentary halt, but in surprisingly quick order she recovered. "Well, keep these youngsters away from Matt until his temperature is down. They ought to be all right. They've probably had the bug, anyway, and it won't get 'em again."

"There's a big sea bass I was going to catch…"

Lillian wasn't listening. She kissed each of the children goodbye, promising that she and their mother would be back before they had even been missed, and that their father would be fine.

"Mind your uncle Drake," she admonished the children as she went out the door.

Drake stared dumbfounded at her departing figure, then his gaze snapped to the youngsters at the table.

Megan's chin puckered.

"Hey, it's going to be all right," he assured her. "Don't cry."

"She cries all the time," Peter said. "Cry-baby, cry-baby!" he taunted.

"Cut that out, Peter!" Toby warned. "She's our little sister."

"Hope Mom doesn't bring home another *giirrrl.*"

Joshua flicked a spoonful of soggy cereal in his older brother's direction. Toby retaliated by hitting the kid with his spoon.

"I'm gonna tell," Peter complained.

"I want my mommy," Megan cried. Tears spilled down her chubby cheeks.

From the other room Matt called, "Dad, can I get up now? I haven't upchucked in a long t-time."

Drake rolled his eyes. This was not how he had expected to spend the day.

WHEN ARIA WALKED into the kitchen, Drake had a little girl hooked on his hip while he was trying to wash her face; two slightly older boys were chasing Buffy under the table; a third boy was stringing fishing line from a cupboard door down the hallway toward Matt's room. Empty cereal bowls, wadded napkins and spilled milk decorated the table.

Repressing a smile, she said a cautious, "Good morning."

He looked a little wild-eyed as he snagged a small boy before he could shut Buffy under the sink. "Lillian's grandkids. She had to go to the mainland."

"I see."

"This is Megan. She's two and a half. The monster boys are Toby, Peter and Josh."

Aria smiled as the little girl buried her face in Drake's neck.

"Hello, Megan. My, but you have pretty dark hair."

"I gotta pee."

"Great," Drake muttered. "Can you hold it just a minute, Megan? I've gotta stop Josh from breaking the VCR."

"Here, I'll take her." Aria held out her arms. With tentative acceptance, Megan leaned toward her.

Shifting the child's weight from himself to Aria, Drake grunted his thanks.

"How long are the children going to be here?" Based on Drake's haggard expression, she hoped Lillian would be back any minute, certainly no more than a half hour. She wasn't sure Drake would survive otherwise.

"Couple of days. Maybe three."

"Oh, dear…"

"Yeah, that's what I thought, only in somewhat stronger language."

She choked down a laugh at the poor man's exasperation. "I guess that means you won't be going out looking for the sea bass for the next few days."

"Not a chance," he grumbled.

A heartfelt sigh escaped her lungs. She'd been given a reprieve, albeit a short one. Perhaps a way to protect Drake from Oceana would come to her before he was free to go fishing again. She fervently hoped so.

He went to rescue the VCR while Aria took charge of Megan. As she ducked under the fishing line strung down the hallway, she met the child she assumed was Toby.

"Interesting technique. What kind of bait are you

using? And what fish are your planning to catch?"
she teased.

"Naw, this isn't for fishing, lady." His tone suggested he didn't think much of Aria's intelligence.
"I got a pulley rigged so Matt can pin a message to
the line and send it into the kitchen. Like if he wants
some more Jell-O or somethin'. Then we can send
him back a message that says it's coming."

"Amazing! That's very clever of you."

In spite of himself, his cheeks pinked with pride
and he stood a little straighter.

Aria suppressed a desire to bend down and kiss
the boy. He was so intense about his invention, she
doubted he would want his masculine pride diluted
by a show of feminine affection.

After she had Megan taken care of and settled
with some crayons and a coloring book, Aria went
to visit Matt. Buffy, somewhat desperately, based on
the way her fur was raised like the spines of a sea
urchin, followed her into the sick room, jumped up
on the bed and burrowed herself out of sight under
the covers.

"How are you, small-fry?" Aria placed her hand
on Matt's forehead and found him cool to the touch.
He was sitting up, and his bed was strewn with toys.
An empty mug sat on the nightstand, along with a
plate that contained a few cracker crumbs.

"I'm okay, but Dad made me have broth for
breakfast. That stuff is yucky."

Something crashed in the living room, and Drake

bellowed, "Stay away from those CDs. They're not for kids."

Aria flinched. She told Matt, "Perhaps your father wants to make sure you are well before you eat any regular food."

"I guess." He shrugged. "He won't let me play with the guys, either. Says they might catch whatever I've got."

"That is possible."

"Then will you tell me another story?"

In a choked voice, Drake cried, "No, Megan, you're not supposed to color the walls."

Aria swallowed back another laugh. The poor man sounded near the breaking point, and it wasn't even noon yet. Though he was clearly well respected in his community, and could no doubt run rings around others in his boat, managing four young children all at once was putting a strain on paternal abilities. As it would any man, she suspected. And most women, too. "I think it would be wise if I told all of the children a story. How would you like that?"

"Wow! Would you? Nobody's mom can tell stories as good as you can!"

A band constricted around Aria's heart, and tears pressed at the back of her eyes. How extraordinarily wonderful to be valued so highly by such a very small person.

It took a while to round up Lillian's grandchildren and get them seated quietly on the floor of Matt's room. Since his temperature was down, Aria guessed there was little chance he was contagious at this point and posed no risk to the other young-sters.

Drake stood in the doorway, for all the world looking like a sentinel guarding against their escape, and Aria found a chair to sit on next to Matt's bed.

"Once upon a time, long ago, in a kingdom be-neath the sea," she began. This time she told the story of a sad sea anemone who was unhappy be-cause he couldn't swim like fish could. All he could do was sit on a rock, waiting for something good to eat to swim by, while the waves splashed him in the face. He pleaded with passing perch and dogfish—the children all laughed at the image of a dog with fins and a tail—but no one would give the restless sea anemone even a short ride on his back. Finally, a killer shark swam by. In fear for their lives, all of the fish fled, but the sea anemone stayed stuck to his rock. The young shark, who didn't like being the neighborhood bully, was so glad to find someone who wouldn't run away, he let the sea anemone climb on his back and took him for the most won-derful ride of his life.

"And ever since," Aria concluded, "sea anem-ones and sharks have been very good friends."

Other than Toby, who was skeptical that fish of any kind made friends with sea anemones, the youngsters appeared content with Aria's tale. Some-what subdued, they went back to their play.

"You are one heck of a storyteller," Drake said admiringly as he kept a wary eye on the youngsters.

"I'm sure it's hard for children to be cooped up inside."

"Yeah, but it's drizzling outside. I hate to send them out in the rain."

Aria glanced through the wide expanse of windows in Drake's living room. The decibel level of the children playing was already rising. Outside, a lowering sky oozed moisture to dampen the dock, but it was hardly enough to be called a rain. Certainly there wasn't enough precipitation to deter merchildren from having fun.

"Do they have jackets with them?" she asked.

"Yeah, I guess."

"What I see outside is liquid sunshine and that never hurt anyone. I think the children should go enjoy it while they can."

Drake's seductive smile and warm chuckle curled through Aria's midsection, heating her in a way the sun never could. "I think you may be one heck of a smart lady."

Aria basked in Drake's praise all afternoon.

The children spent the time building forts of driftwood on the beach and warding off alien invaders. When the sun finally came out, and Matt appeared recovered from his bout with stomach flu, Drake let his son join the others.

Nowhere in her memory could Aria recall a more exhilarating day, or one that had been quite so exhausting.

When they finally got the children tucked in for the night, she collapsed onto the couch, leaned her head back and closed her eyes. Being human—particularly, filling in for an absent mother—was harder than swimming against a fast-flowing current.

She felt Drake's weight settle beside her, but she didn't bother to open her eyes.

"Quite a day, huh?" he asked.

"Has it only been one day?" she countered. "It feels like a hundred." Her back and legs ached in an unfamiliar way; her head continued to throb with the lingering reverberations of children at play.

"That Toby is a real pistol, isn't he?" Drake said. "He set up that booby trap with a bucket of water on top of the doorway, and damned if I didn't fall for it. I swear, if he'd been my kid, I would have tanned his hide good."

"You showed great restraint, Drake. Particularly when that bucket ended up on your head."

"Well, I couldn't get the darn thing off. *Somebody*," he said pointedly, his dark eyes narrowing with mock severity, "could have helped me out if she hadn't been so busy laughing."

She giggled. "I'm sorry."

"No you're not. But next time—God, I hope there isn't any next time for that particular stunt." The low rumble of his laughter vibrated through the couch, and she felt it both physically and as an echo of the longing in her heart. The sensation intensified when his arm looped around her shoulder. She relished the feeling. Instinctively her head drifted to rest on his broad shoulder.

As he rubbed his cheek across the crown of her

head, his afternoon whiskers tugged gently on her hair.

"I hope Lillian's son-in-law is all right," she said. She was floating on a cushion of fatigue mixed with sensual pleasure, an odd combination that was strangely comforting.

"I hope his recovery sets a speed record. I don't think I can handle many days of this much stress."

She snuggled a little closer, burrowing into his masculine scent and letting its sweet potency invade all her senses. "The children love you. All of them."

"Yeah, maybe."

"Could we take them to the village tomorrow?"

"Hmm, good idea. At least it would distract them for a little while." Drake gazed out the living-room window, as content in this moment as he could ever remember being. The glow from the floodlight at the end of the dock caught a misting rain like so many diamonds reflecting against the black velvet of the night. The woman beside him smelled of the sea, fresh and zesty, arousing him in ways he hadn't thought possible. She'd been like a rock with the kids today. And each time she'd calmed a crying child or mended a skinned knee, he'd wondered at her nurturing abilities.

Maybe Matt was right. Maybe he should start considering Aria as a possible *real* mother for his son.

Her breathing eased into the steady rhythm of sleep.

Drake smiled. She either trusted him completely, to be so relaxed in his arms, or he'd totally lost his sex appeal. He'd like to think it was the former.

Clenching his teeth, he fought the unwelcome tautness in his body.

After a while, he found his own eyes drooping closed. Moving carefully so he wouldn't wake Aria, he tugged a crocheted afghan off the back of the couch and spread it over them both, adjusting their positions so they were entwined like lovers sated after they had expended their passion.

"I think tomorrow, while we're in town," she said with yawn, "I'll see if I can find someone who will agree to get me pregnant."

Chapter Ten

Drake fell off the couch.

"You're going to do *what?*" he bellowed.

Shaking the curling tendrils of mental seaweed away, Aria sat up. Apparently, in that moment between wakefulness and sleep, she'd spoken her dreamy thoughts aloud. Now she had little hope of calling them back, or of Drake understanding her need. Nor was she particularly enthusiastic about her plan. She would much rather Drake be the one to start a baby growing in her belly—a sweet, dark-eyed child like Matt. But that didn't appear to be a choice.

"Shh. You'll wake the children."

"Forget the damn children." He finally lowered his voice to a harsh whisper. "What's all this talk about getting pregnant?"

"It's the only thing I can do. I need to get pregnant, and you've made me see very clearly that I have no right to force you to father a child you don't want. So I simply have to find someone who isn't quite so touchy on the subject of who he gets pregnant.''

"Who he gets…Aria, you're talking like your reel is a yard short of being full. Women *need* to get pregnant like they *need* a toothache.''

"In my case, it's a matter of life and death.''

"How can you say something like that? Life and death? You've gotta be kidding.''

In spite of the sense of failure that twisted through her chest, she lifted her chin. "Quite the opposite. I am very serious.''

"The whole idea's crazy! You can't walk up to some guy and ask him to, well, you know.''

"I'm trying to be as reasonable as possible under the circumstances.'' Reasonable, considering that her need was urgent and she'd much prefer Drake to father her child than anyone else she could imagine.

"You never said…I mean…you did it with me so you could get pregnant?''

"It must have been obvious that I was upset about you using a T-R-O-J-A-N.''

"Yeah, right. You don't have to spell it, Aria.'' He sat on the edge of the coffee table and plowed his fingers through his hair. This conversation was part of a bad dream. It had to be. Women didn't have sex for the sole reason of getting pregnant. And what the devil did that say about her feelings for him? Was he nothing more than a handy sperm bank? "Why the devil are you so anxious to get pregnant?''

"Since the act won't concern you, I'd prefer not to explain my reasons in detail. I wouldn't want you to feel obligated to do something you'd otherwise refuse to do. That wouldn't be fair."

"*Fair?*" Temper simmering near the boiling point, he lifted a skeptical eyebrow. "I see. You want to hook some poor sucker into marrying you, and you're going to do that by getting pregnant. And you know damn well I wouldn't fall for that line a second time, not after my experience with Janie."

"Janie?" She looked genuinely puzzled. "This doesn't have anything to do with your wife."

"Oh, no? It sounds like the same ploy to me. She wanted to get away from her parents in the worst way. Getting pregnant and talking me into marrying her was her ticket out of the house. Then she found out she'd hopped a train that didn't go any farther than Hart's Cove."

Her chin jutted up a notch. "This seems a fine destination, but I wouldn't expect marriage at all. Just pregnancy."

She looked so damn sincere, Drake could almost believe she was telling the truth.

Almost.

In spite of himself, his gaze lowered to her abdomen. He pictured her slender figure full and ripe with a baby growing inside her—*some other guy's baby.* He ground his teeth.

"The other night, when you and I...if I hadn't had any condoms—" He gestured vaguely.

"I was hoping you would take care of matters for

me, but now I understand your reluctance. Truly I do."

He nearly choked. "So do you have someone in particular in mind to, ah, do it?"

"I'm not sure it matters much." She shrugged. "I thought I'd see who was at the general store tomorrow, when we take the children to the village. Surely one of your friends here on the island would be willing to help me out."

Help her out? She made it sound like a charity event.

Drake swallowed back a vow that Aria wouldn't ever get any closer to the general store than she was right now. Not in *his* lifetime. And sure as hell not when any of his "friends" were around. Particularly that over-eager Joe Voulgan, with his solid diet of oysters.

"Just what is it you plan to do after one of my so-called 'friends' gets you—" Words escaped him. Damn, he hadn't thought Aria would be like this. *Like Janie.* At least she was more up front about her scheme.

She stood and stretched, rotating her shoulders as if she was stiff from sitting on the couch too long. Or from chasing after kids all day. "I'm not exactly sure. I guess I'll deal with that problem later. *If* I get pregnant in time." She yawned broadly.

If, hell! All she had to do was ask one guy and he'd be so hot he'd be cooking in about twenty seconds.

"It's getting late," she said. "I think I'll go to bed now."

From another woman it might have sounded like an invitation. From Aria it didn't. She'd already decided some other guy was going to be the one to get her pregnant. Further, she appeared absolutely content with that decision.

Hell's fire!

"I'll walk you up to your cabin."

She studied him, her eyes heavy with the need for sleep. Sexy eyes. Bedroom eyes. "I don't think that's a good idea. You might be tempted to—"

"No. I won't be."

"The children—"

"They're all sound asleep. Nobody will miss me."

"One of them might wake up. This is an unfamiliar house for Lillian's grandchildren. I wouldn't want them to be frightened without an adult around to reassure them."

Drake's natural reserve and sense of responsibility warred with a far more basic instinct. He knew exactly what would happen if he walked Aria up the bluff to her cabin. It'd be hours before he got back to the house again—hours of hot, sweaty passion and sheer orgasmic pleasure. He'd likely forget all about his principles, and have a hell of a good time doing it.

But the end result would be catastrophic, forcing him into a marriage he hadn't planned. And in the meantime, while he was off indulging in his baser instincts, one of Lillian's grandkids might wake up and need him.

The choice was more difficult than he'd expected. He swallowed hard. "Well, yell if you need me."

She smiled, and he wondered if there wasn't a bit of sadness in the way her full lips quivered before she turned away. She left the house by the back door.

He was ready to follow her, in spite of his best intentions, but a kid in the other room made a crying sound. As he went to see what was wrong, he told himself it was better this way. No entanglements.

"Yeah, sure," he muttered.

"COME ON, D-DAD. Everybody's ready to g-go."

Drake slid the thirty-foot measuring stick into the holding tank to check how much gasoline he had on hand, a fueling service he provided for boaters. He'd been up since before dawn. In fact, he'd hardly slept at all after Aria's announcement last night that she intended to get pregnant. What kind of a fool idea was that? he wanted to know.

"We're not going anywhere," he told his son.

"S-sure we are. Aria said we're all going to the village."

"Nope."

"But Aria said you p-promised."

He hefted the pole out of the tank. The liquid stain of gasoline showed the tank was three-quarters full, just like he expected. "Sorry, son, I've got other things to do today."

Matt's expression crumbled in disappointment. Drake felt like a jerk. It wasn't his concern that Aria was set on having a baby. He didn't want anything to do with it. *Not his problem.*

Lillian's grandkids came running toward the fueling area behind the toolshed, little Megan trying desperately to keep up with her big brothers, but her legs were too short and she ran well behind the rest of the pack.

"He says we're not going," Matt related.

"How come?" Toby asked. His siblings gathered around him.

"He says he's too busy."

Five sets of big brown eyes questioned Drake's integrity—plus one pair of accusing green eyes, when Aria joined the shrimp-sized lobbyists.

"I promised the children," she said. "If you cannot take us, then I will walk to the lighthouse. James won't mind, I'm sure."

Ah, hell! James would probably try to do anything Aria asked of him—including stuff he was too damn old to even be thinking about. Drake didn't want him saving Aria a trip to the village.

With a muttered curse, Drake set the measuring stick aside and locked the lid closed on the gasoline storage tank. "*I'll* take you into the village." But he damn well wasn't going to let Aria out of his sight.

HE'D STUCK TO HER like a tenacious barnacle for the past hour, ever since they'd driven into the village.

Aria didn't know what to do. Every time she began to consider a likely prospect who might assist with her problem, Drake was right there. Interfering!

"Hugh Penweather is sterile," Drake told her about a man with long arms and a narrow face who was sitting on the porch of the general store.

"Sterile?"

"Yeah, he can't have children. Mumps as a teenager did him in. Terrible thing," he said solemnly.

"Oh." She frowned. The man looked healthy enough, but she supposed something like that might not show.

Matt and his friends had gone off to play at the community center down the street, where there was a very good day-care facility for Megan, as well as good supervision for the older kids. There were shrieks of laughter coming from the grassy field out front. Occasionally a ball bounced into view only to be quickly retrieved by one of the youngsters.

She eyed an older man leaning against a battered pickup. Dressed in overalls, a cigarette dangling from his mouth, he didn't hold much appeal. But she was desperate. In less than ten days, the full moon would rise. She could almost feel scales growing on her legs.

"Toliver's wife would kill him," Drake warned in a low voice.

Aria's eyes widened. She wouldn't want to be responsible for that.

Apparently the task she'd set for herself was far more complex than she had envisioned. First Drake had made it clear—justifiably, in his view—that he didn't wish to father her child. Now she discovered that identifying a substitute to perform the deed was fraught with all sorts of obstacles, not the least of which was the fact that no other man she had met held any serious appeal.

Before she reached the steps to the general store, Drake caught Aria's arm. He felt like he'd spent the past hour in a liar's contest—Toliver's wife had moved to the mainland a couple of years ago and they were divorced. Hugh Penweather already had a houseful of kids. Drake supposed Hugh's wife wouldn't be all that keen on loaning her husband to help with Aria's project, even if they were no longer the ideal married couple.

Drake had simply been telling Aria whatever came to his mind. Clearly his thinking was about as jumbled as a plate of spaghetti. His nerves felt just as tangled.

"Why don't we have a nice quiet cup of coffee while the kids are playing?" he suggested, subtly directing her toward the restaurant instead of the general store. He'd already spotted Lampert's boat at the dock, figured he was in the store jawing with Dudley, and didn't want to risk Aria putting Chuck on her list of possible suitors. Not his best friend.

She glanced toward the store, then at Drake. "If you'd like."

He didn't much like the resigned sigh he heard. A guy wanted to think he was the best choice around, for coffee or anything else.

An overnight rain had left the street muddy, and he had to veer around a puddle. When he glanced up, he saw Willy Williams coming out of his office down the street. The police officer waved Drake over. He was frowning and had several official-looking pieces of paper in his hand.

The timing was lousy, but Drake didn't have much of a choice. "Look, wait here for me, would you, Aria? I've got to see the local constable. I won't be long."

In an unhurried gesture of remarkable grace, she shifted her long tumble of silver-blond curls to the front of her shoulder. "Of course, I'll wait on the porch."

Drake took a final look around. Except for Toliver—and Willie—the street was empty of prospects for Aria. It ought to be safe enough to leave her for a minute.

With a few quick strides, he closed the distance to Willy.

"Since when did you turn into a practical joker?" Willy asked in none too friendly fashion.

"What do you mean?"

"I got the report back on those fingerprints you wanted me to check out."

"Oh?" Drake got an uneasy feeling in the small of his back. He turned and spotted Lampert talking with Aria. *Damn.* Apparently Chuck had wandered out of the store and found Aria by herself. Drake knew he shouldn't care what she did or with whom. She wasn't his problem. But he did care. Too much.

And he sure didn't want her to get hooked up with his best friend—not for this kind of favor.

"Drake, are you listening to me?"

He turned back to Willy. "Huh?"

"I said the authorities couldn't get any match on those fingerprints on the glass you gave me. They didn't even think they were human—not the right kind of swirls. If you were trying to play a joke on me—"

"No, no. Nothing like that. I probably smeared them, or something." Distractedly, Drake waved off the accusation. He didn't have time to deal with fingerprints right now. Smooth-talkin' Lampert was hitting on Aria, and from the smile on her face he guessed she was damn well enjoying it. "Look, I gotta go. Thanks for checking, anyway."

ARIA'S HEART SANK a little deeper into the pit of her stomach with each minute she talked to Chuck Lampert. Secretly she had hoped he would be the one. But now she was sure that wouldn't be possible.

Oh, he was a very nice man. Quite handsome in a boyish way that didn't compare to Drake's darkly brooding good looks. And he made her laugh. But in spite of her desperate need to mate with a human male, she could not imagine sharing with Chuck the same intimacies she had shared with Drake. She couldn't ask him. The words simply wouldn't come.

Nor did she think Chuck would consider doing the deed unless Drake gave him specific permission.

Based on this morning's experience, that seemed unlikely.

"So, if you ever want to take a ride with a *real* fisherman," Chuck concluded after relating a rollicking funny story of having simultaneously hooked on to three fish with one fishing line, "I'm your man."

With a trace of bittersweet sadness, she took in his lazy grin, knowing she much preferred Drake's expressive eyebrows and more reluctant smile. "Thank you. I'll certainly keep that in mind."

He opened his mouth to say something, but closed it again when Drake arrived and placed a blatantly possessive hand at the small of her back. His palm heated through her sweater.

"Chuck's *not* your man, Aria," he said tautly.

Her head whipped up, and her gaze met eyes dark with anger.

Ignoring her surprised reaction, Drake said, "We better check on the kids."

"Hey, Drake, I thought you'd be out beating the water for that big sea bass."

"Something came up. But I'll land it one of these days."

"I was just trying to talk Aria into going fishing with me. Maybe she'll bring me good luck, and I'll be the one to hook into that bass."

"She's not available." Taking Aria's arm, Drake propelled her down the street, wondering what the devil had gotten into him. Chuck was just making friendly conversation. And he'd acted like he was a jealous lover protecting his best girl. His best buddy whom he trusted implicitly.

Yeah. Maybe.

Best friend or not, no way did he want Chuck Lampert—or any other man—to volunteer to help Aria get pregnant. The whole idea was crazy. Surely she would come to her senses soon and realize that whatever she was running away from, or hiding, would fix itself without the necessity of such an extreme measure. Getting pregnant never solved any problem for a woman, as Janie had certainly discovered.

As he walked with Aria down the street, his arm hooked across her shoulders, he decided he'd have to come to her rescue. Not by getting her pregnant, he told himself piously. He'd use a rational, problem-solving approach. But he needed a little time. He couldn't have her hopping from one guy's bed to another while he was trying to work out a serious solution to whatever dilemma she faced.

Nope.

He would have to convince her that he'd cooperate with her stated objective. Then he'd use delaying tactics till she came to her senses.

Admittedly he would be misleading her. *Lying.* But dammit! It was for her own good.

Armed with a plan—at least a strategy to delay any irreversible action on her part—the tension eased from his shoulders and his stride became more relaxed.

"So, Aria, did you find anybody who sparked your fancy?"

She canted him a puzzled look. "My fancy?"

"You know, did you find any likely candidates for, ah, you know?"

"Oh. That." She shook her head, feeling more discouraged than she had since she'd discovered she had legs. "Not really."

"Well, don't worry about it. I think I can solve your problem for you."

She came to an abrupt halt. "You can?"

"I figure since we've already...you know...and we're pretty compatible—"

"You're willing to get me pregnant?"

He shrugged. "You're still interested?"

Her heart did a fair imitation of a porpoise leaping in an aerial somersault. "Yes, I'm interested."

"Fine. That's good." He cleared his throat. "Then, ah..."

"Now?" Her gaze darted around the village in search of somewhere they could be alone.

Embarrassed heat raced up Drake's neck at the same time his groin tightened. "Well, we can't exactly do it here in the middle of the street."

"No, I guess not." Aria briefly considered his Jeep as a possibility, but it didn't seem like a comfortable one.

"We'll work things out," he promised expansively. His arm weighed heavily—intimately—around her shoulders as he gave her a squeeze.

His gesture echoed in a tightening band around her heart. "When we get back to Hart's Cove?"

"We can't do much with Lil's grandkids around. We'd never be sure of having any privacy. But after they leave—"

"That's only a few more days, isn't it?"

"A couple. That's all."

She could wait that long. The full moon wouldn't appear for more than a week. There'd be plenty of time remaining for Drake to get her pregnant after the children had returned to their own home.

Anticipation thrummed through her. Her whole body reacted, from the tips of her breasts to the low, curling heat that sped through her midsection.

The next two days would seem like an eternity.

Chapter Eleven

The past two days had been hell.

Today was worse.

Aria watched him like a big fish getting ready to pounce on a little fish. Every time Drake glanced in her direction, she smiled at him slyly.

Knowingly.

Then he got an instant image of her buck naked in his arms that made him groan and set his teeth on edge.

His forceful physical reaction—combined with a matching emotional reaction he couldn't seem to dispel—made him wish he had a pair of jeans a good two sizes larger than the ones he was wearing. In fact, being aroused had become a permanent—and painful—state, both physically and mentally.

He felt like an idiot hiding in the toolshed while the kids built driftwood forts on the beach, but he didn't know how much more of this sweet torture he could stand.

He heard the squeak of hinges as the door opened. Greeting him with an eagerness that stole his breath,

Aria captured him between the work bench and her sweet, sexy body, her arms sliding around his mid-section.

"Perhaps something dreadful has happened to Lillian," she said, all but purring like an affectionate cat. "Do you think we should try to call her in Vancouver?"

Her pert breasts pressed against his chest, sending a surge of heat rocketing toward his groin. "No, I don't think so," he managed to say. "Where are the kids?"

"They're all in the house. Toby has them all making a big Welcome Home sign for Lillian. She should have returned by now."

"Sometimes these things take longer than we expect." But not long enough that Aria had given up her idea of getting pregnant.

She rested her head against his shoulder. "I suppose you're right," she sighed. "But I am anxious to…you know."

Instinctively he rubbed his cheek across the crown of her head. His afternoon whiskers rasped against the silvery strands, sandpaper on silk. Cursing his own weakness, he inhaled her fresh, sea air scent. "I thought by now you'd be having second thoughts about—"

"Oh, no, not at all. I'm more eager than ever."

He stifled a groan as her talented fingers kneaded the taut muscles that knotted in his back. "Getting pregnant isn't something you do on a whim, Aria."

"I'm well aware of that."

"It's a life-changing experience."

She hummed another sigh. "More than you know. But I'm sure it will be for the best."

"It's an eighteen-year commitment. Maybe longer."

"That sounds wonderful."

Drake remembered Janie had claimed to be in love with the idea of motherhood, too. But she'd hated it and couldn't wait to leave her baby behind while she went off to pursue her own kind of fun. This time he wasn't going to fall for sweet-talkin' words. Six months. A man needed that long to really get to know a woman. Minimum.

He took Aria by the shoulders and forced her to step back. "Whatever problem you've got, Aria, there has to be some other solution."

Like a bolt of lightning on the open sea, a flash of pain arced through the depths of her eyes. "You've changed your mind, haven't you?"

"I just think it would be smarter—"

"I don't have much time left, Drake. Either you do this for me, or I'll have to—"

He cut off her threat in the only way he knew how. He crushed his mouth to hers. He didn't want to hear her say she'd sleep with some other guy.

The sensual electricity of her kiss jolted him, like bringing two live wires together. It drove any further hope of rational thought from his mind. Angling his head, he deepened the kiss, coaxing her lips open. He plunged his tongue inside to taste and explore secret ridges and hidden valleys.

Her response was almost innocent in her eagerness and the quick sigh of surrender. She gave him unrestrained access to all he cared to take.

He slid his hand down her back, splaying his fingers over the soft swell of her hips. He groaned as she pressed into the nest of his pelvis. Fine tremors shook through his body.

How could he ignore this mind-numbing need that she incited with so little effort? How could he not want her? How could he not take her? Now. Here. In the toolshed amid broken bits of equipment, worn outboard motors and broken fishing nets.

With no way to take precautions against an unintended pregnancy, he thought with another groan.

"Aria! Drake! I've come back to rescue you from my four little monster grandchildren!"

Lillian's call was like a wave of ice water washing over Drake—just what he needed. He gulped a breath of air, his heart pounding like an out-of-sync propeller.

Aria didn't look any too steady herself. Her glossy lips were damp with his kiss, her eyes as dark as the sea on a cloudy day. Her chest shuddered as she drew in a breath. Finally a smile quivered at the corners of her kiss-swollen lips.

"Lillian's back," she said.

"Sounds like it."

Her smile broadened victoriously. "Then tonight's the night?"

Reality slammed into Drake's gut. He'd been playing the fool thinking Aria would come to her senses. How the devil was he going to get out of this one? Assuming he still wanted to.

Tunneling his fingers through his hair, he stubbornly renewed his vow to not be taken in by a woman who was looking for easy answers.

"Land's sake, you two." Standing outside the shed, Lillian squinted and peered into the shadows. "This the only place you could get yourselves some privacy?"

Heat stole up Drake's neck. "I had some work to do out here."

Her perceptive, dark-eyed gaze darted from Drake to Aria and back again. "Imagine it's nice work if you can get it," she said with a hearty laugh.

"How is your son-in-law?" Aria asked smoothly, as if they hadn't just been caught in a compromising position.

"Oh, he's gonna be just fine. My girl took him on home, and I'm here to pick up the youngsters."

"There's no rush," Drake suggested.

"I'm gonna take Matt with me, too. I figure after the better part of four days with five kids underfoot, you two could use a little time to yourselves."

"No!" Drake nearly choked on his hurried refusal.

"How sweet of you, Lillian." Smiling, Aria glanced up at Drake with those drop-dead, sexy, bedroom eyes. "The children haven't been a bother, but I'm sure Matt would be happy to spend more time with his friends."

Drake tried desperately to get out another objection. But his throat was so constricted, he couldn't manage a single word. He could barely breathe. *Tonight's the night!*

Nodding, Lillian said, "I'll go round up the youngsters. I'll keep 'em all at my house tonight and bring Matt back in the morning. You two can, ah, finish up whatever I interrupted, if you want."

As she walked away, Drake heard her chuckling in what could only be described as diabolic glee. Lil thought another woman had trapped him into marriage just the way Janie had.

He thought otherwise.

Before going to the house to pack a bag for Matt's overnight stay with Lillian, he made a hurried stop at his boat, dropping into the cabin for just a moment. Reassured by the box he tucked in his jacket pocket, he headed back up the dock, his steps jaunty.

He'd pleasure Aria in every way possible, satisfy her as only a man could, but he wouldn't allow either of them to make a mistake they might all too soon regret.

ARIA LIFTED a second morsel of oyster from the can and dropped it into her mouth. Chewing the flavorful bite, she swallowed and licked her lips.

"You sure you don't want some?" she asked Drake, sliding the can toward him across the kitchen table.

"No. I'm fine with this." He bit into the hamburger he'd fixed himself for dinner. A line of juice squirted out the edge of the bun and he used a napkin to wipe his lips.

With a mental sigh, Aria envied that fragile piece of paper the intimate contact it enjoyed with Drake's full lips.

The house was eerily quiet after four days of rafter-to-rafter children. In the silence she could hear the lap of waves hissing rhythmically across the rocky shoreline; the dock creaked as it echoed the movement of the shifting sea. Somewhere nearby a loon called its mate home.

"I miss the children," she said wistfully. "I mean, I'm glad we have this time together so we can...you know...but it does seem awfully quiet, doesn't it?"

As he took another bite, he nodded in agreement.

"Do you suppose we can do it in one try? Or will it take more than once?"

He choked on his hamburger and coughed. His dark-hued complexion turned a dusky shade of red.

Aria patted him on his back. "Are you all right?"

"Yes. Fine." His eyes springing tears, he downed half a glass of milk, then drew a deep breath.

"So, what do you think? Will once be enough?" she repeated.

"If the timing's right, that's all it takes."

Aria puzzled over that as she ate another oyster and munched on a bun. She knew little about the mating cycle of human females. Failure was a risk she didn't dare take. Certainly trying extrahard would not be an onerous burden, but rather a pleasurable one.

Looking across the table, she smiled brightly. "I think we ought to do it as many times as possible between now and when Matt comes home in the morning. That way we'll be sure."

Drake started coughing again, so hard this time, he had to get up from the table and leave the room. Aria sincerely hoped he wasn't coming down with something. A delay at this late date due to his incapacity, could spell disaster for her.

She straightened up the kitchen, washing the dishes they'd used for supper and piling them on the drain board. When Drake still hadn't returned, she went in search of him.

She saw him standing on the porch, staring out beyond the cove to the open straits. A mist had begun to fall. In the faint light, raindrops shimmered on his dark hair like crystaline pearls. His broad shoulders, lean hips and long, tapered legs gave him the look of a sea god risen to survey his watery domain. His stance was wide, as though he was standing on the bridge of some grand ship, ready to meet the challenge of whatever weather Father Neptune chose to unleash on him.

Drake simply took her breath away. Her heart, too, she realized, for she had fallen in love with a noble man who gained his living honestly from the sea.

She stepped out onto the porch to join him.

Without turning toward her, Drake said, "I'm a

weak man, Aria." His softly spoken words were like the whisper of waves against a far shore.

"I find you very strong."

"I want you so much it hurts."

Joy squeezed a tight band around her heart. "Then let me ease your pain."

When he turned, she went into his arms.

For an eternal moment, Drake simply held Aria, fighting a battle he knew he would lose. And then, in desperation, he surrendered to the mountainous need that engulfed him.

He scooped her into his arms and carried her to his bedroom, as he had that first night when he'd found her on the boundary rock. He wanted her like that again. Naked, her hair spread across his pillow, her scent filling his nostrils, her image permanently imprinted in his mind.

"I want to touch you," she whispered, her fingers deftly unbuttoning his shirt.

"Yes," he groaned. In contrast, his efforts felt clumsy as he removed her sweater, then lowered her tight-fitting jeans over her hips and down her slender legs. He nuzzled the triangle of silver-blond curls he found there.

Together they fell onto the bed, rolling and kissing, arms and legs wrapping around each other.

"Drake..." Her breath caught on his name. "It feels...so..."

"Yes, sweetheart. So good." He kissed her face, her cheeks, the sensitive column of her neck. He was a fool, he admitted, but a cautious one. He kissed her face until her eyes closed, then reached for the box of condoms in the drawer beside the bed. He was going to have to hurry. Her uninhibited response had him racing to the peak too fast, too soon.

He yanked the condom from the foil envelope, slid it on his—

The damn thing came apart in his hand!

He swore under his breath.

"What's wrong?" She rolled her head from side to side, her lips brushing past his mouth in a hot, wet caress.

"Nothing," he said with a grunt, reaching for another packet.

She arched against him. "Now, my darling. Please."

Frantically, using only one hand as he continued to caress her delicate breasts with his other hand, he positioned the condom and rolled—

A ring! A lousy ring, not a rubber at all.

My, God! He was panting so hard, he was hyperventilating. He was going to explode any second. He'd never suspected, not for a second, that the packets had been tampered with. He'd been in such a hurry, so damn eager and wanting. Beyond noticing…

Clenching his teeth, he knew there was no hope for it. He'd have to call on every last drop of his willpower. Sweat trickled down his forehead.

He entered her with a quick thrust. She sobbed his name and bucked beneath him. She plowed her fingers through his hair and drew him closer.

Instantly he felt the ripple of her fulfillment squeezing him, trying to drain him of every last drop of his good sense. He wanted to let go. God help him, he did. But once before he'd been forced into marriage by his carelessness. He didn't have the strength to pay that penalty a second time, no matter how passionate he felt at the moment. No matter how deeply he cared about Aria.

This time he wanted to be one hundred percent sure of what he was doing. With Aria it was too soon. There were too many questions, too many secrets.

And she felt too damn good!

As the eruption began, he groaned in frustration and pulled back to spill his seed on the sweat-dampened sheet between her legs.

ARIA LAY VERY QUIETLY, her breathing settling into a more even rhythm. Drake had already rolled away, though she could hear his breath, even more raspy than hers. Their only physical connection was his hand splayed across her stomach.

Something was seriously wrong.

She scooted up in the bed and searched for the light switch on the bed lamp. The glare made her squint.

There on the sheet was the evidence of Drake's betrayal—foil packets and shredded bits of rubber T-R-O-J-A-N she had ravaged in the hope of saving her own life. The damp stain between her legs was further proof that he had lied to her.

Her woman's heart wept bitter tears. She had given her love; he had deceived her.

"You never intended to get me pregnant."

An angry wind from the north announced the arrival of a storm, rattling the windows. Gooseflesh rose on Aria's arms.

"I wanted you, Aria. More than I ever thought possible."

Her chin quivered. She pursed her lips tightly and blinked her eyes closed against the burning tears. His desire wasn't enough to save her. She ached for opportunity lost.

She realized he hadn't moved. Nor had he met her gaze. In spite of the jagged pain of his treachery that was threatening to tear her heart apart, she reached out to brush a straying lock of dark hair away from his forehead. She longed to feel the silken strands again, to weave her fingers through the lush thickness. One last time.

But he had deluded her into believing that he cared, too. Instead he'd mortally betrayed her.

Denying herself that final caress, she squirmed off the bed and picked her clothes up off the floor.

"Where are you going?" he asked. He had a beautiful body, lean and strong, darkly furred across his chest and arrowing down to the nest of his manhood. His salty taste still lingered on her tongue.

"Away."

"It's late. There's a storm coming."

An arctic blast that would drain the strength of a

mermaid, just as a broken heart wore down the endurance of a woman. "It doesn't matter."

"You can stay. We'll talk in the morning."

"You don't understand. Soon it will be too late. If I do not become pregnant, I may die before spring and warm weather returns."

"You're talking crazy, Aria." He patted the bed beside him. "Come back to bed. We'll talk…"

Lifting her chin, she left the room with the dignity born of being the daughter of a king who had led his merpeople wisely, until he, too, had been betrayed by another.

FOR MOST OF THE NIGHT she huddled beneath a fir tree at the end of the point. The wind swept curtains of rain across the water, stirring the surface of the normally calm straits to a boil of whitecaps.

As the dawn tried vainly to pierce the veil of clouds, the soaring song of a mermaid rose to meet the storm. Oceana wove uncanny strains of melody through the hissing whitecaps and drove her notes higher and higher, challenging the power of the churning sea, daring sailors to follow her wherever she would lead.

Immune to the lure of her wicked stepmother, Aria still felt the determined tug of Oceana's vocal seduction. It plucked at an elemental need to be one with the sea, one with the very essence of life that had begun so long ago beneath the vast expanse of water that covered the earth. The fact that this song had the power to drive men crazy did not surprise

Aria, for in Drake's arms she, too, had teetered near the precipice of insanity.

Shivering, she pulled her coat—soft as sealskin—more tightly around her. She ignored the dampness on her cheeks that could have been raindrops...or tears.

In the shifting wind it was difficult to gauge where Oceana lurked among the swells and low-lying rocks that edged Oyster Island. And Oceana was her most dangerous when she lay in wait to ambush an unwary sailor.

DRAKE HAD STARED at the ceiling for most of the night and listened to the wind lash the rain against the windows of his bedroom.

He'd hurt Aria. He'd broken the promise he'd made to her. He'd lied to her so she wouldn't go to some other man with her nutty scheme. From the beginning, he'd known he was wrong to deceive her. But he hadn't been able to stop himself.

He hadn't even tried.

And now she'd left him. He could hardly blame her. It was better this way, he'd told himself over and over, though it was an unconvincing lie.

The gray light of dawn was just edging in through the window when he heard her singing. It was a heartbreaking sound. The melody tormented his conscience. He'd caused her so much distress that the only way she could express her pain was through a heart-wrenching song.

His fault.

Somehow he had to make amends, get her to understand his past mistakes demanded that he not make a hasty commitment again.

In return, he had to get her to explain in a way he could comprehend why getting pregnant was so damn important to her.

Dressing quickly, he grabbed his yellow rain slicker and hat from the rack. Outside, wind drove rain into his face. Even though he could hear her song, trying to spot Aria was like looking through a waterfall.

Feeling increasingly uneasy, he followed the sound of Aria's voice—or at least he thought it was her singing. It seemed to pulled him onward, almost luring him against his will, toward the end of the dock.

And then he saw her, the distinctive flash of her blond hair through the gloom and rain.

She was in a dingy at the entrance to Hart's Cove. The small outboard motor was no match for the angry straits when a storm was running. The boat bobbed in the waves. The wind drove the boat like driftwood, precariously close to the rocks and potential disaster.

Drake's thoughtless behavior had driven her to this desperate moment.

"Aria!" he shouted, but the wind whipped his call back into his face. He waved his arms and called out to her again.

She returned his wave, beckoning to him, then turned the boat and headed it out into the straits, as if she was courting death...and wanted him to follow.

"My God!" he groaned. What was she thinking?

He raced for his Boston Whaler, untied her and leaped on board. He had to reach Aria before her tiny boat capsized and she was lost in the churning sea. He wouldn't be able to bear the weight of guilt if she died because of his callous treatment.

The engine responded to his command. He prayed he would catch up with Aria in time.

BENEATH THE SOUND of the wind, Aria heard the throb of an engine. She snapped her attention toward Hart's Cove and Drake's departing boat.

Fear gripped her heart like the arm of an octopus determined to squeeze the life out of its prey. Suddenly, drawing a simple breath was painful.

She leaped to her feet. "No!" she cried. Waving her arms, she burst from the shelter of the trees. Raindrops that had clung to the branches spattered her face.

"Drake! Don't go!" The wind snatched her cry away.

From the corner of her eye, she caught sight of a small boat and the distinctive blond hair of a mermaid. Hair the same shade as her own.

Oceana! Where had her stepmother gotten a boat? Aria wondered frantically.

Swinging the prow around, Drake maneuvered his boat to follow the tempting lure. Oceana had cleverly drawn Drake from the safety of his harbor by pretending she was Aria.

Aria's stomach knotted in fear.

Unable to attract Drake's attention, Aria raced up the path. She had to get help. Though he had betrayed her, she still loved him and always would. It wasn't his fault he couldn't understand the ways of merpeople, and she'd been too afraid of his rejection to tell him. But she could not let Oceana lead him to his death.

Half running, half sliding, she plunged onto the dirt road that ran the length of the island. Stumbling, she fell to her knees in the mud. The blood pumping through her veins filled her head with a roaring sound. She gasped for breath.

A horn blared so close, she jumped.

"Land sakes, Aria!" James peered out the window of his battered truck. "What are you doing running around in the rain?"

"Thank goodness you're here." She struggled to her feet. The roaring she'd heard had been the engine in James's truck, not her imagination.

"I was coming to see Drake. That fool Salmon Woman stole my dingy. Saw her flop herself right in, I tell you, tail and all. Then damned if she didn't start up the motor and go puttering off by herself. I want Drake to go after her. Darn thieving woman."

"Drake's not here." Aria pulled open the door on the passenger side. "Hurry, James. Take me into the village. Take me to Chuck Lampert."

Chapter Twelve

Chuck shook his head in dismay. "You mean Drake has gone out fishing in *this* weather? He's gotta be crazy."

"Please, there's no time for explanations," Aria pleaded. James had taken her to Chuck's home not far from Oyster Bay. She'd obviously awakened him, and he was still buttoning his shirt as he talked to her. "We've got to save him before he does something terribly foolish. It's life and death."

"He's gone after that sea bass, hasn't he? Shoot, that guy would do anything to get his trophy, instead of mine, mounted on Dudley's wall. As if it made a hill of beans difference."

Rainwater dripping from her hair, she tugged at Chuck's arm. "There's no time to waste." The wind howled around the house as if to emphasize the point.

Chuck grabbed his jacket. "I oughta let him get himself out of whatever mess he's gotten into. No fish is worth risking your life for in this kind of weather."

"He's your friend."

"Yeah." He eyed Aria critically. "And you love him, don't you?"

She didn't hesitate. "More than my own life."

"Lucky guy."

Chuck went with her to James's truck and climbed in after her. The motor was still running.

"I'm going to need an extra hand in this weather, James," Chuck said. "Think you're up to it?"

"You bet." He shifted gears and the truck lurched forward.

"I'm going with you, too," Aria insisted.

"I never thought otherwise." He gave her a reassuring smile. "We'll find him."

THE BOW LIFTED and dropped with a bone-jarring crash as they raced through the wind-whipped waves that churned the straits. Aria's stomach echoed the sensation. A mixture of rain and seawater pelted the windshield, splaying across the glass and blurring their vision. The deck was so deep in water, they were up to their ankles in runoff.

"Do you see him yet?" Chuck shouted over the throbbing scream of the engines. He clung to the wheel as if their lives depended upon it. Aria suspected they did.

James gave a shake of his rain-soaked head, his gray hair plastered flat to his scalp. "Not yet."

Aria peered through the storm. They were riding blind, but Chuck had assured her no other boats would be out in this weather. There could be other debris, however, like floating logs and flotsam churned up by the waves. Every mermaid knew the dangers of violent weather. Aria suspected Oceana had taken this dreadful risk because she was so filled with hatred that only vengeance would satisfy her evil appetite.

"There!" James pointed toward the north, toward the narrows.

Chuck swore. "What the hell has gotten into Drake? The tide's about to shift."

"That's dangerous."

"In this weather, there'll be whirlpools during the exchange, sure as my name's Lampert. It'd take a fool to try to get through those narrows now."

Or a man lured by an evil mermaid who was unfamiliar with these waters and the dangers they posed. "We've got to stop him," she cried.

"I'll try." He shoved the throttle forward. The engines protested even as they responded. "This would be a hell of a time to blow a gasket."

Terror constricted Aria's chest. She could barely draw a breath. Drake couldn't die. She simply wouldn't let that happen, whatever the cost to herself.

Slowly they closed the distance to Drake's boat. And then, beyond his Boston Whaler, Aria spotted the tiny dingy. At that instant a wave caught the smaller craft. The bow flipped it into the air and, for a moment, Aria saw the terrified face of her stepmother and heard the keening cry of mortal fear.

Oceana hadn't known how unusually dangerous

these waters could be. That much was obvious as she tumbled into the swirling sea.

The breath lodged in Aria's throat.

Cursing, Chuck shouted, "What the hell is Drake up to now?"

Aria watched the man she loved toss a sea anchor over the stern of his boat. Then, in an act of foolish heroics, he dived over the side to save Oceana.

The sea swallowed him in a second and Aria cried, "No, Drake!"

She didn't pause to think any more than he had. The whirlpool that formed with the changing tides tossed waves over itself, swirling and twirling and dragging each bit of flotsam down into its vortex. Aria knew only that she loved Drake. She forgot she was no longer a mermaid with a powerful tail that could propel her away from dangerous currents. She forgot that icy water drained her of strength, in the same way it had drawn the vitality from her wicked stepmother, whose head bobbed briefly above the surface of the angry sea only to vanish again, leaving a wail of terror.

Taking only a moment to push off her shoes and shed her jacket, Aria dived into the water. She would save Drake or give up her own life trying.

Icy cold enveloped her. She struggled through the frigid water, diving deeper and deeper in her search for Drake. Her arms were still strong from stroking through the sea as a mermaid, her lungs still powerful enough to endure long minutes below the surface. Unlike Oceana, she had not been drained of strength by an added month in these chilled waters. The current and tide buffeted her, but she fought back.

Below her, she spied the twirling, futilely struggling form of a man.

She dived deeper. Stretching herself to her limits, she reached out to him, snagging his shirt collar. With a furious, determined kick, she sought the surface. Her lungs burned. Salt stung her eyes. Her arms felt as weak as a baby's, and she rued the absence of a powerful tail to catapult her upward to safety.

They breached the surface together. She gasped for air. He coughed and she rejoiced. Drake was alive!

"I've got you, Aria!" Between hacking breaths, he struggled in her arms. "You're okay now."

Treading water, she smiled and held her lover's head above surging waves. And he held her. The whirlpool had spit them up from the black depths. They both lived. It was enough.

A life preserver landed with a splash beside her. She hooked Drake's arm through it, along with her own, letting Chuck haul them to safety on board his boat.

ARIA'S TEETH CHATTERED and shivers racked her body.

"You two get below deck and get out of those wet clothes," Chuck ordered. Engaging the throttle, he steered a course away from the narrows to quieter waters. "You'll find some blankets above the bunk."

"What about my boat?" Drake's body convulsed with the same chill that shook Aria. "Did it go aground? Or get sucked into the whirlpool?"

"Nope. I came alongside and put James on board before I spotted you and hauled you two out of the drink."

"Thanks, buddy. Glad you came along." He gave Chuck a friendly slap on the back. "I owe you."

"You got that straight. You musta been smokin' some damn strange stuff to come out fishing in this weather."

"Yeah, something like that." He shot Aria a crooked grin and hooked his arm over her shoulders. "Let's get changed."

Her legs wobbly from the cold, Aria ducked her head and dropped down into the cabin. Escaping the wind and pounding rain helped to warm her, but she still felt chilled to the bone.

Drake snatched a blanket from the bunk and scrubbed her hair dry.

"You're c-cold, too," she stammered, trying to use a corner of the blanket to mop the water from his face.

"I'm okay."

They both undressed, wrapped themselves in dry blankets, and Aria curled her feet up under her on the bunk while Drake put water on the stove to boil for coffee. When that was done, he handed her a steaming mug and took one for himself. He sat down next to her.

"I know I upset you last night, Aria, and I apologize. God, I didn't mean to hurt you. But what on earth made you take that dingy out in this weather? Didn't you know how dangerous it could be?" He skimmed his fingertips over her cheek. "Were you that desperate that you wanted to run away from me?"

She closed her fingers around the welcome warmth of the mug and looked up into the dark sincerity of his eyes. There'd never be another man she could love as much as she loved Drake. "It wasn't me you were chasing."

"Not you? But I saw you and heard you singing."

"That was my stepmother."

"I thought you didn't have any family."

"She's not someone I'd choose to be related to. She was luring you to what she hoped would be your death. Instead, it's very likely she's the one who died." At least, Aria thought that's what had happened. Oceana must have misjudged how much of her strength had been drained by the cold northern waters and had lacked the energy to fight that whirlpool.

"I don't understand. I'd know your hair color anywhere. I saw you going out in the dingy."

"It was James's dingy you saw. Oceana had stolen it. Her hair is very similar to mine."

His eyes narrowed and he became defensive. "You're the one I pulled from the water."

Shaking her head, she told him how she had been sitting on the point when he left the cove in pursuit of Oceana, that she'd gone for help, found James and eventually convinced Chuck to search for him.

Drake drained his coffee mug and stared at her incredulously. "Why would your stepmother want to *lure* me anywhere? I've never even met the woman."

"For revenge. After she banished me from our village of merpeople, the others turned on her and drove her away. She followed me here, planning to get even with me."

"Wait a minute." He held up his hand, thinking he must have misunderstood her. *"Merpeople?"*

"Oceana is...*was* a mermaid." In a self-conscious gesture she traced the design on her mug. Then, so softly Drake couldn't be sure he'd heard correctly, she said, "So am I."

When her words finally registered, a thousand impossible thoughts and images popped into Drake's mind. The night he'd found Aria on the boundary rock at Hart's Cove. His son's bizarre fascination with mermaids. Aria's inability to read or even open a can of oysters, as if she had come from some other world. Her indecipherable fingerprints. And finally—the most telling of all—the quick flash of a silver tail as the woman he'd been pursuing flipped out of the skiff, flew into the water and was quickly sucked into the whirlpool. A tail with the same configuration as a giant sea bass and the body of a beautiful woman with long blond hair.

A mermaid!

"Oh, my God..." His gaze snapped to Aria's legs. Two feet and a beautifully shaped calf peeked out from beneath the blanket. It wasn't possible...

"It's a peculiarity of mermaids that if we come out of the water during a full moon, we are transformed into a human."

"Transformed?" he asked stupidly. His brain cells must have suffered oxygen deprivation while he was underwater. None of this made sense. He'd made love to a mermaid? Twice? And he hadn't noticed? She'd wrapped her legs around his waist. *Two legs,* for God's sake! Not a tail. How could they have even done it if she'd had a tail?

He ground his teeth. The night he'd rescued her, there'd been a full moon—a transforming moon.

"I was reluctant to tell you."

His hand shook as he set his coffee mug aside. "I can understand that."

"I wasn't sure how you'd react."

How did a man react? Aria a mermaid? It made just enough bizarre sense, filled in just enough of the puzzle pieces about who Aria was, that Drake believed her. He had to. But it was going to drive him crazy.

The sound of the engines slowed.

Chuck pounded on the hatch to get their attention. "We're coming into Hart's Cove now. Looks like James got your boat back here safe and sound."

That, at least, was a blessing. It meant Drake still had a way to earn his livelihood.

He cleared his throat. "Does, ah, anyone else know? About you being, ah…"

"Mermaid," she supplied. "Matt saw me once with my tail. James obviously spotted Oceana—more than once—but he's convinced she was the Salmon Woman."

"That's good. Real good." He stood, careful not to bump his head on the ceiling. "Why don't we sort of keep this as our little secret for now?"

"Of course." Wrapping the blanket securely around her, Aria followed Drake up the steps to the deck. She'd seen the stunned disbelief in his eyes. And then…sweet Neptune, had his feelings turned to revulsion?

There was no need to tell him how she might retain her human form. He'd been so obviously shocked by her revelation, he wouldn't be interested in sharing his milt with her now. Indeed he was probably most grateful that he had taken precautions to prevent impregnating her.

Tears stung at the back of her eyes, and her throat clogged with emotion. She shivered as a gust of wind caught the hem of the blanket.

How many more days until a full moon? Too few, she realized in anguished despair.

"D-Dad! Aria!" Matt ran toward them from the house. "Lillian brought me home and nobody was here!"

Drake met his son on the dock and awkwardly scooped him into his arms, trying not to drop the blanket in the process and expose himself. "We're here now.'' He was acutely aware of Aria getting off the boat right behind him, relieved that Chuck was there to provide her with the necessary assistance. He didn't know what to say to her; didn't know if he could even look her in the eye.

A mermaid.

As he carried the boy back toward the house, Drake acknowledged James on the deck of his boat with a grateful nod, figuring he'd check things out more thoroughly after he got some clothes on. Though nothing was showing, he felt more exposed at the moment than he could ever recall.

''She stole my dingy, you know,'' James grumbled. ''It'll be nothing but driftwood now.''

''Sorry.'' With other concerns on his mind, Drake had a little trouble sympathizing with James's lost boat. Later he'd find a way to make it up to the old man.

Matt hooked his arm around Drake's neck and hitched himself up. ''Hey, how come you don't gots any clothes on?''

''We had a little accident, that's all.'' He'd accidentally discovered the woman he'd been sleeping with was a mermaid. One without a tail.

''So you went swimming?''

''Not exactly on purpose.''

Matt's eyebrows wobbled and his face scrunched up in confusion. ''Aria, too?''

''She didn't mean to, either.'' Why had she ended up in the water, he suddenly wondered. If he'd dived in after the imposter—her stepmother—then why hadn't Aria stayed high and dry, maybe tossing him a life preserver like Chuck had? Who, he wondered belatedly, had rescued whom?

"Lil said grown-ups need time to be together without little k-kids around. You 'n Aria were together last night."

"Yeah, we were."

As he entered the kitchen, Lil eyed him and the drooping blanket speculatively. He set his son down and hiked up the blanket again.

"I figure the whole village will be interested to hear this story," Lillian said with a chuckle. "How 'bout giving me first crack at spreading the word?"

"Not on your life." He'd just as soon his swim in the straits didn't make the five-o'clock news, not even in Oyster Bay where Chuck was sure to repeat what had happened—as far as he knew it. More than that, he hoped to escape even the mention of the word *mermaid.*

Following him down the hallway, Matt skip-hopped into his bedroom and somersaulted onto the unmade bed—the bed where Drake had made love to Aria last night. The sweet, hot memory shot straight to his groin.

She had *two* legs, dammit!

"So, since you and Aria spent the night together, does that mean she's gonna be my m-mom?"

Drake's hand froze on the pair of jeans he'd reached for in the closet. "What makes you think she's going to be your mother?"

"Lil said maybe so."

"Lillian ought to mind her own business." He pulled on the jeans and reached for a shirt.

"I think she'd make a good mom. Don't you?"

A picture of Aria attending a school parents' night came to him, her arm tucked through his as she balanced on her tail and hopped to the front of the classroom to meet the teacher. He stifled a groan. "I don't think so, son."

Matt sat cross-legged in the middle of the bed. "She tells real g-good stories."

"Yeah, well, there's more to being a mother than telling stories." Like being *normal*, for God's sake. A *mermaid?* How was he supposed to deal with that? "Let's talk about it later, little chip. I've gotta check on my boat now. Okay?"

The boy flopped onto his back with his arms outstretched as if he was landing on a trampoline. "Okay. But I still think Aria would make a good m-mom."

When he went back into the kitchen, Drake found Aria talking to Lillian. Still wrapped in a blanket, her tumble of curly hair filled with damp tangles, she looked small and delicate and incredibly vulnerable. How could anyone so sexy be anything but all woman?

"I gotta check on my boat," he told them gruffly. He eased by Aria without meeting her gaze for fear of what he'd see in her eyes. Hurt? Betrayal? Certainly temptation. Even knowing the truth about Aria, he wouldn't be able to resist her.

With new understanding, he realized why men of

the sea had always told tales of sailors following the siren songs of mermaids to their deaths. If Aria was any example, mermaids were darn hard to resist.

THE DOOR CLOSED behind Drake's departing figure, and Aria expelled a sigh.

"What's been going on?" Lillian asked. "I thought you and Drake would be takin' advantage of not having any youngsters underfoot. Didn't figure you two would be out fishing."

"We weren't. Not exactly." She tunneled her fingers through her tangled hair.

Lillian's brows leveled, and her dark eyes filled with concern. "Why does it sound like the course of young love isn't running too smoothly?"

Aria flushed. "He doesn't love me." How could a human male love a mermaid? It was an unnatural thing, one member of a species loving a member of another. Except that she loved Drake.

"Funny. I sure thought you two were getting on together. Of course, Drake can be stubborn."

"Very." Think how often she had tried to seduce him—and failed.

"You mark my words, honey, you'll wear him down. No red-blooded fella like Drake could resist you for long."

But Aria wouldn't be able to stay at Hart's Cove much longer. Remaining near the straits, and the predator fish it harbored, would be too dangerous for a mermaid made weak and lethargic by the chilled waters. To be safe, she would have to go somewhere else before her tail reappeared.

Her heart nearly broke at the thought of leaving Drake and his son. Whatever loneliness she had experienced before would only be magnified, having found, and lost, her one true love.

Matt trudged into the kitchen, his expression a replica of his father's and his tiny fists jammed into his pockets.

Aria swallowed the tears that threatened. "What's wrong, small-fry?"

"I thought I had it all figured out."

"What's that?" She cupped the back of his head.

Matt looked up at her, his gaze as solemn as that of the old man of the sea. "I thought if I asked Dad real nice, he'd make you my mom."

A lump formed in Aria's throat, so thick she wasn't sure she would ever be able to speak again. "What did he say?"

"He said we could talk about it later. But I want you to be my mom *now*. All the other guys have a mother, but I don't gots one. I never have, not since I was real little. And I don't even remember her."

Kneeling and cradling Matt's sweet, serious face between her hands, she struggled to find the right words that would help him. And all the while her heart was shattering into pieces so small she knew she'd never be able to put them back together again. "I think that's the nicest thing anyone has ever said to me. There's nothing I'd like better than to be your mother, but I'm not sure I can be."

"I'd be real good," he promised. His chin quivered.

She pulled him into her arms and hugged him so tight he complained. "I love you, small-fry. Whatever happens, promise me you'll remember that I love you."

"I guess."

She looked up and through the blur of tears she saw Lillian. Their gaze met and held, and she knew the older woman would be her ally if only she could develop a plan that would make Drake accept who and what she was. At this point that seemed an unlikely possibility.

WITH LILLIAN BACK to spending much of her time helping her daughter, the days that followed fell into an odd pattern of denial. Drake didn't ask Aria to leave, nor did he mention her revelation that she was a mermaid. It was as though he was tiptoeing barefoot through a bed of razor-sharp coral and, as long as no one said the word *mermaid,* he could walk through unscathed.

But he watched her. He couldn't help himself.

When she walked into a room, he noted the grace with which she moved, the perfect shape of her legs and the womanly swell of her hips. He remembered the warm, satiny feel of her skin, and the safe harbor he had found in her arms.

He envied the quick smiles she flashed for Matt, the glimpses he saw of what a good wife and mother she'd be, and ached because he could see nothing but bleakness in her sea green eyes.

As he poured himself a second cup of morning coffee, there was a knock on the back door. Matt had gone to his room after breakfast, and Aria was quietly going about cleaning up the dishes. They didn't talk much any more. Drake couldn't figure out what to say.

He opened the door.

"Morning, Drake. Aria." Willy Wallace removed his cap as he stepped into the room. "Thought you'd both like to hear what washed up on Quadra Island after that last big storm."

Aria stopped what she was doing, the bowl she'd been washing frozen in her hands.

"What's that?" Drake asked casually.

"It wasn't a very pretty sight."

Aria's heart rate accelerated.

"A woman washed onto the rocks, or more like a half a woman."

Gasping, Aria let the bowl slip from her hands. It clattered onto the tile countertop.

"Do they know who she was?" Drake asked.

"The authorities haven't identified her yet. It's not going to be easy since it looks like she'd been in the water for some time. Could be that missing woman from Nanaimo." Willy fiddled with the brim of his cap. "Funny thing is, half a big sea bass washed up with her. The medical people think that there might have been a big shark out there feeding, and the storm made him a little crazed. That would account for the two halves they found."

Closing her eyes and dragging in a painful breath, Aria knew there was another explanation. Oceana's bid for vengeance had killed her. Any threat she had once posed for Aria was finally gone forever. But it was a tragic ending she would have wished for no one.

"Maybe that was the sea bass everyone spotted and was out to catch," Drake suggested.

"Could be," Willy agreed. "Looks like there won't be a new record catch mounted at Dudley's store for a while."

Drake lifted his hip onto the corner of the breakfast table and slid Aria a look. "Somehow that doesn't seem to matter anymore. Not to me, anyway."

THAT EVENING, from the bluff above Drake's house, Aria watched the moon rise and knew she had delayed as long as she could. It was time to leave Hart's Cove. By the following night at this hour, the moon would be full—and she would regain her beautiful silver tail.

A tail she no longer desired.

Chapter Thirteen

"What do you mean, she's gone?" Drake raged.

Lillian planted both of her fists on her ample hips. "What part of *gone* don't you understand? Aria's left and she's not planning to come back anytime soon."

"It's your fault." Matt mimicked Lillian's rebellious stance. "I wanted her to be my mom."

"She can't be your mother. She's a—" Drake bit off the word. He'd left early that morning to go fishing and do a little thinking on his own. When he'd returned, he'd found the house empty. Lillian and his son had only just come in from wherever they had been, and it was already late afternoon. He'd been frantic with worry. "Where did she go?"

"She asked me to take her into the village."

"Then she hasn't gone far." Relief surged through him. As impossible as it seemed, deep in Drake's gut he hoped this whole mermaid business had been a bad dream. "Look, she didn't even say goodbye. I'm sure she'll be back."

"She told *me* goodbye," Matt asserted. His chin wobbled. "She cried, and so did I."

"I bawled my eyes out myself. That's a sweet girl, and you did something that made her set on leaving." Shaking a finger in Drake's direction, she made clear what she thought of him. "You ought to be ashamed of yourself."

A sudden sharp pain twisted through Drake's gut. Aria had really left him. Deserted him when maybe they could have still worked things out. Gone without telling him goodbye.

Lillian snatched up the dirty dishes from the table and dropped them none to quietly into the sink. "Chuck Lampert agreed to help her out."

"Chuck?" Drake's voice caught in surprise. "What's he gonna do?"

"I imagine whatever it was you *wouldn't* do for her."

He stared at Lillian incredulously. What he wouldn't do for Aria was get her pregnant. He'd drawn the line there. Firmly. His best friend, the buddy who he'd grown up with, wouldn't step in and do that in his place.

Would he?

Drake began to sweat.

Besides, he thought Aria had lost interest in that particular project. She hadn't said a word about it since she announced she was a... Even the word stuck in his gullet. Why would she slip back into that old groove again?

Except it had seemed terribly important to her at

that time that she get pregnant. With *his* help—or some other guy's.

Buffy hopped up onto the kitchen table and meowed loudly. He leveled the cat a reproachful look. Yellow eyes glared back at him as if the disappearance of her new friend—a friendly *mermaid*—was his fault.

"See, Dad? Even Buffy's mad at you."

"Yeah, right." Damn, what an insane four weeks this had been!

"It's all right, Matt." Lillian sniffed in disapproval. "Chuck is a fine young man, and I'm sure he'll do whatever needs doing to take care of Aria. Even if your father is too pigheaded and just plain stubborn to do it for himself."

An image of Chuck making slow, languorous love to Aria popped into Drake's head. The two of them making love *often* enough and *long* enough to make sure Aria got pregnant. And of her *enjoying* it.

His hands clenched into fists. Damn friendship! He'd kill the guy!

He grabbed his jacket from the coatrack.

"Where are you going?" Lillian asked.

"Out."

"How long will you be gone?"

"As long as it takes."

AS LONG AS IT TAKES to do what? he wondered as he cast off the lines to his boat. Because of the condition of the island road after the recent rains, it was faster to get to Oyster Bay by boat than by car. And he was in a hurry. A big hurry.

He was still unsure of what he was going to do, when he marched up to the general store looking for Chuck. He was sitting on the porch, his chair tipped back as if he didn't have a care in the world, whittling.

"Where is she?"

With an unhurried stroke, Chuck slivered a piece of wood. "Wondered how long it would take you to get here."

"Don't mess with me, Lampert. I want to know where Aria is." And what she's doing—and with whom.

"I don't see that it's any of your business. She has a right to leave the island if she wants."

"She's left the island? Where did she go?" Drake had figured she'd be here in the village—trying to get pregnant.

"I think if she'd wanted you to know, she would have told you herself."

"What if I make it my business to find out where she is?"

"Why would you want to do that?"

"Because—" Because his kid wanted Aria to be his mother and because he wanted her—mermaid or not—to be his wife. The realization was so startling, like a bolt of lightning cutting through the darkest night, that Drake's knees buckled. He sat heavily on the porch steps. "Because I love her." Admittedly he hadn't known her for six months. Not even six weeks. But it didn't matter. He *knew*, dammit! He loved Aria.

Slowly Chuck lowered his chair to all four legs. "Why didn't you say so before, man?"

"I didn't know." And now it was too late. She was gone.

"I took her to Sechelt."

Drake's head snapped up. "To the marina there?"

"Nope. She wanted to go to the provincial marine park. Wouldn't tell me why."

Frowning, Drake thought maybe he knew why. She had chosen to go to the one place where she knew there was a mermaid, albeit a statue. She'd gone there because she was going to transform back into a mermaid herself.

He buried his face in his hands. God, what could he do now?

"She said something about a full moon, but she sure didn't seem very happy about it. Poor kid. I tried to get her to stay with me."

"No!" Drake leaped to his feet.

"Hey, man, don't jump down my throat. You're the one who let her get away. I have this real strong feeling she didn't want to go, and she wasn't willing to stay and settle for second best." He shrugged. "If I was you, I'd go after her and see if I could change her mind…about a lot of things."

Chuck was right. Drake had to try. He had the distinctly uncomfortable feeling that if he failed tonight, it might be too late.

Emotion tightened his throat. "Thanks for helping her, Chuck."

"No problem, buddy." He pondered the slab of wood he'd been whittling. "There is another kind of screwy thing you maybe oughta know, though."

"What's that?"

"She didn't take a suitcase, but she took a whole case of canned oysters with her. And one of those hand-crank can openers."

HE CUT THE ENGINE and let the boat glide into the mirror-calm water of the sheltered cove. There wasn't much underwater vegetation here and few fish. A mermaid would risk starvation without a food source of her own. Like canned oysters.

Aria could have gone south to a warmer climate, he realized, or chosen waters that had far more abundant fish life. In fact, Chuck could have flown her to any destination she wanted.

But she'd elected to stay here. Not all that far from Hart's Cove. Drake hoped that meant something. But he'd been wrong before about a woman. He was afraid to trust his judgment now.

It was almost dark. An evening fog had caught in the tops of the hemlocks and firs, misting them like a surrealist painting. Somewhere in the forest a woodpecker attacked a tree trunk in search of dinner. The air was rich with the combined scent of damp soil, lush ferns and the sea.

The prow gently nudged the bluff. There was no sign of Aria. No sound.

Drake leaped ashore and tied a line to a tree.

Then he spotted the case of oysters tucked under a picnic table near the water line, within easy reach of a mermaid who had to come out of the water to eat.

"You might as well show yourself, Aria. I know you're here."

There was a rustle of leaves, branches parted and Aria appeared.

Drake nearly collapsed in relief to see she still had legs. Two of them.

Emotion tightened his throat and made his voice rough. "You didn't say goodbye."

"I didn't think you'd care."

"I care. More than I ever thought possible."

She closed her eyes and sighed. "It's too late, Drake."

Not wanting to spook her into flight, he cautiously edged closer. "Maybe it's not too late. If you tell me why you came here to Sechelt."

She shook her head.

"It has something to do with you transforming back into a mermaid—and needing to get pregnant before there's a full moon. Am I right?" He didn't understand all the details, but he'd put that much of the puzzle together. And it scared him nearly to death.

When her silence confirmed what he'd guessed was true, he cupped her chin. "Why didn't you tell me?"

Tears sparkled in her eyes. "Because you're so

noble, you would have done something you didn't want to do."

"Like get you pregnant? That doesn't sound like such a terrible thing."

"You don't want me to have your baby. You never did."

"Maybe I've changed my mind."

"I'm a mermaid."

"Right now you're a woman. The woman I love."

Her eyes widened. "Love?"

"I admit I'm a little slow to catch on. But now I realize I've loved you since I rescued you from the boundary rock at Hart's Cove. But you scared me, Aria. I've never felt so out of control. I didn't know how to react."

She palmed his cheek in a warm caress. "And now it's too late."

"Tell me what I have to do. Anything, Aria. I love you so much, I can't stand the thought of losing you." Turning his head, he placed a soft kiss in her palm. She tasted of salt and passion remembered. "Besides, Matt's madder than hell at me. So mad that when he bawled me out, he didn't even stutter. He wants you for his mom."

In spite of her tears, she smiled. "I'd like nothing better than to be his mother. But to do that, I have to be permanently transformed into a human."

"What does it take?"

"Before the full moon rises tonight, I have to become pregnant with the milt of a human male. I'm not sure that's possible in such a short time."

He looked up at the dark sky where stars were beginning to show through the clouds. Moonrise was only a few hours away. There wasn't much time. "We could try."

"And if we fail? I'll be a mermaid again."

"Then I'll take you back home with me, tail and all."

"I can't remain out of the water for long, Drake. My scales grow too dry."

"I've got a big bathtub. We'll manage. I can even bring in salt water if that that's what you need."

She cocked her head. "You'd do that? You'd keep me with you even if I was a mermaid?"

"I'll do whatever it takes to have you where I can love you and take care of you. If you turn into a mermaid tonight, so be it. On the next full moon, you'll transform into a human and we'll try again. And we'll keep doing that until, by God, there's a baby. *My baby* growing inside you. However long it takes."

The tears that had been threatening edged down her cheeks. "Oh, Drake, I want your child so much. Only yours."

Her admission was the only excuse he needed. He enveloped her in his arms. She felt small and fragile, yet he knew she was a strong woman. "You saved my life, didn't you? I would have drowned if you hadn't jumped in the water after me."

"I guess I forgot I'd lost my tail."

"You could have died."

"Without you, my life has no meaning. I love you, Drake Hart."

Elation surged through him. With Aria's love, he was invincible.

He claimed her mouth with a kiss that was meant to seal their bargain. He would protect her and care for her. In return she would love him. That's all he'd ask; that's all he wanted. Her love.

Breaking the kiss, he framed her face between his hands. His breathing was labored. "I think we better get started."

"No more T-R-O-"

"None." He picked her up in his arms and carried her to the boat, lifting her onto the deck as if she were precious cargo. He hopped on board right behind her. The boat rocked with their sudden weight.

"I'm sorry I ruined your condoms," she said. "I was just so upset that you didn't want to get me pregnant. I didn't understand how important that act was to you."

"I would have been smarter if I'd really listened to why it was so important to you to have a baby—life and death. I could have saved us both a lot of grief."

Below deck, she turned into his arms. Trembles of excitement and fear shook her body. "I'm afraid, Drake. What if this doesn't work? I've never actually known a mermaid who transformed—"

He cut off her qualms with another kiss, and she gave herself over to his bold conviction that all would be well. The boat lifted on a gentle swell as he undressed her. Her garments fell to the floor in a soft, sibilant sound like the whisper of the sea caressing a distant shore.

When his jacket and jeans and undergarments had joined her clothing in a heap, he pressed her down onto the narrow bunk.

He rained kisses all over her body, searing her with a heat that came as much from inside her flesh as from the warmth of his lips. His tongue traced a vivid pattern along her sensitive inner thigh. Her legs trembled and she whimpered a long, intense sound of joy and hope.

"Oh, Drake..." She thread her fingers through the thickness of his hair. Her body shook as he found acutely responsive places, secret places she hadn't known existed until Drake had taught her of their pleasures.

Giddy with anticipation, she knew after this night she would never be the same no matter the outcome. Human or mermaid, she loved Drake and he loved her. That, in itself, was transforming.

He rose above her, bracing himself. A fine tremor shimmered through his arms and shoulders as he pressed himself forward, through the slickness that welcomed him. Their gazes locked.

"This is forever," he whispered.

"Forever and beyond."

Her body stretched to accommodate him, the sliding friction a sweet heat. She lifted her hips to him. The sensation of their being one, in heart, mind and body, was life altering. She was his, he was hers. Man and woman. Her love. Her mate.

"I love—" his voice caught as he drove into her more deeply "—you."

A glorious force shattered her. Like the beauty of a tropical sunrise, the power of wind-driven waves to alter the shape of the land.

Sobbing, her hands moved convulsively over his shoulders and down his sweat-slicked back. Her chaotic contractions triggered his explosive release. He filled her, changed her and made her whole.

Their passion ebbed as they lay curled in each others' embrace, but the tension of what might come next kept their heartbeats pounding. The boat rocked; the line linking them to the shore creaked in a matching rhythm that mocked their fears.

"Hold me, Drake," she pleaded. Her senses focused on her legs, the clawing fear of scales moving up flesh that had now become a part of her. A comfortable part. Human. She twitched and her breath caught. "Please…"

"You're mine, Aria. Whatever happens." With his arms wrapped around her, he represented strength and power. But could he ward off her return to a life she had once known?

Reaching across her, Drake slid aside the curtains that covered the small window above the bunk.

He swore a low, anxious curse. "We're turned the wrong way. I can't see—"

"Is it moonrise yet?"

"Damn, I don't know." In desperation, he pulled

her even more tightly into his arms. He would not lose her. His love. His life.

The boat swayed on a shifting tide. He held his breath.

"Look, Aria, the moon."

The bright yellow circle—larger than any moon he had ever seen—filled the sky. Wispy clouds played a leisurely game of tag with the few stars that hadn't been eclipsed by the glow.

He let his hand drift down across Aria's flat belly, past the triangle of soft curls at the apex of her thighs. He stroked her legs. A woman, he thought with satisfaction. *His* woman, who would bear his child.

He smiled proudly, as if only he had the power to create new life. "Think we ought to start coming up with names for the baby?"

Her body shook with laughter or sobs, he couldn't be sure which.

"That can probably wait." She laughed lightly in an echo of the relief he felt, and she rolled onto her side, facing him. She kissed his chest and teased his nipple with her tongue. "Right now I want to make sure we haven't overlooked some important detail. I wouldn't want my transformation to reverse itself if we did something wrong."

His body reacted to her clever tongue and he groaned. "Hadn't thought of that." But he was certainly glad Aria had, because he wanted them to make love again, too. Just to make sure they'd done everything right.

Epilogue

Nine months later

Aria handed two-day-old Caprice to Drake, then let him help her over the side of the boat onto the dock at Hart's Cove. It was good to be home from the hospital on the mainland, but she felt none too steady on her feet.

"Mom! Dad!" Matt raced out of the house toward them. It was a beautiful summer day, and from the swim trunks he was wearing, it looked as if he'd been taking full advantage of the warm weather.

Kneeling, her heart filled with pride and love, Aria accepted a welcome home hug from her son. "How are you, small-fry? I missed you."

"I beat Tommy swimming this morning," Matt said, his speech free of any trace of a stutter, as it had been since the day Aria married his father.

"Good for you," Aria kissed her son lightly.

"Can I see the baby? Can I?"

"Sure, son," Drake said. "But let's get your mom inside where she can sit down."

They walked up the dock, Matt hopping up and down so he could get a better look at Caprice. Aria was relieved. She'd been afraid Matt might experience some jealousy of the baby. Instead he seemed quite eager to meet his sister.

Lillian met them at the door. "Oh, my, what a sweet thing," she crooned to the baby in Drake's arms.

"I suppose you're gonna claim rights as honorary grandmother," he said with mock gruffness, giving Lillian a wink.

"You can bet your life on it, young man." She brushed her lips to Caprice's forehead.

"Drake and I wouldn't have it any other way." Aria gave her a quick hug as she went inside. Lillian beamed with pleasure.

In the living room Aria sat down at the end of the couch, took the precious bundle from Drake and patted the cushion beside her. "Come on, small-fry. Sit next to me and I'll let you hold Caprice."

He hopped up and scooted all the way back until his legs stuck straight out. "She doesn't have much hair."

"She'll grow more." At the moment, Caprice's cap of dark hair lay in tiny ringlets around her head, promising her mother's curls in the future. She peered around her strange new world with her father's dark brown eyes.

Aria passed the baby to Matt. "Hold her head up. Her neck isn't very strong yet."

"Can I see her? Really see her?"

"You mean you want me to unwrap the blanket?"

"Just for a minute."

Puzzled, Aria did as her son asked.

"Aw, gee!" Matt complained, staring at the squirming baby. "She's got *legs!*"

Aria stifled a laugh. "Of course she does. What did you expect?"

His small face scrunched up in grim disappointment, his expressive brows leveling. "I bet Tommy twenty-five cents she'd have a *tail!* Now he's gonna think I'm a real dork."

To disguise her amusement, she hugged her two children in one big embrace. Her gaze locked with Drake's across the room. Grinning, the proud papa mouthed the words, "I love you."

Her soaring heart echoed the same sentiment. No mermaid could have found more happiness than she had as a woman.

Take 4 bestselling love stories FREE

Plus get a FREE surprise gift!

162

**From the bestselling author
of *Jury Duty***

Laura Van Wormer

It's New York City's most sought-after address—a prestigious boulevard resplendent with majestic mansions and impressive apartments. But hidden behind the beauty and perfection of this neighborhood, with its wealthy and famous residents, are the often destructive forces of lies and secrets, envy and undeniable temptations.

Step on to...

RIVERSIDE DRIVE

MIRA
BOOKS

**Available in January 1998—
where books are sold.**

Free Gift Offer

As Seen on TV!

With a Free Gift proof-of-purchase
from any Harlequin® book, you can receive
a beautiful cubic zirconia pendant.

This stunning marquise-shaped stone is a genuine cubic
zirconia—accented by an 18" gold tone necklace.
(Approximate retail value $19.95)

Send for yours today...
compliments of ❦HARLEQUIN®

To receive your free gift, a cubic zirconia pendant, send us one original proof-of-purchase, photocopies not accepted, from the back of any Harlequin Romance®, Harlequin Presents®, Harlequin Temptation®, Harlequin Superromance®, Harlequin Love & Laughter®, Harlequin Intrigue®, Harlequin American Romance®, or Harlequin Historicals® title available at your favorite retail outlet, together with the Free Gift Certificate, plus a check or money order for $1.65 u.s./$2.15 can. (do not send cash) to cover postage and handling, payable to Harlequin Free Gift Offer. We will send you the specified gift. Allow 6 to 8 weeks for delivery. Offer good until March 31, 1998, or while quantities last. Offer valid in the U.S. and Canada only.

Free Gift Certificate

Name: _____

Address: _____

City: _____ State/Province: _____ Zip/Postal Code: _____

Mail this certificate, one proof-of-purchase and a check or money order for postage and handling to: HARLEQUIN FREE GIFT OFFER 1998. In the U.S.: 3010 Walden Avenue, P.O. Box 9071, Buffalo NY 14269-9057. In Canada: P.O. Box 604, Fort Erie, Ontario L2Z 5X3.

FREE GIFT OFFER   084-KEZ

ONE PROOF-OF-PURCHASE
To collect your fabulous FREE GIFT, a cubic zirconia pendant, you must include this
original proof-of-purchase for each gift with the properly completed Free Gift Certificate.

084-KEZR2

Prepare yourself for the Harlequin American Romance Blizzard of 1998!

Question:

What happens when a runaway bride, a young mother and a schoolteacher on a field trip with seven little girls get stranded in a blizzard?

Answer:

Not to worry, they'll each have a hot-blooded man to wrap them in sizzling male heat till the thaw—and forever after!

This winter cozy up with **Cathy Gillen Thacker's** new trilogy of romantic comedies for a case of cabin fever you'll never want to cure.

BRIDES, BABIES & Blizzards

Snowbound Bride (#713)
February 1998

Hot Chocolate Honeymoon (#717)
March 1998

Snow Baby (#721)
April 1998

Available wherever Harlequin books are sold.

BESTSELLING AUTHORS
IN THE SPOTLIGHT

.WE'RE SHINING THE SPOTLIGHT ON SIX OF OUR STARS!

Harlequin and Silhouette have selected stories from several of their bestselling authors to give you six sensational reads. These star-powered romances are bound to please!

THERE'S A PRICE TO PAY FOR STARDOM... AND IT'S LOW

$1.99 U.S.
$2.50 CAN.
Special Offer

As a special offer, these six outstanding books are available from Harlequin and Silhouette for only $1.99 in the U.S. and $2.50 in Canada. Watch for these titles:

At the Midnight Hour—**Alicia Scott**

Joshua and the Cowgirl—**Sherryl Woods**

Another Whirlwind Courtship—**Barbara Boswell**

Madeleine's Cowboy—**Kristine Rolofson**

Her Sister's Baby—**Janice Kay Johnson**

One and One Makes Three—**Muriel Jensen**

Available in March 1998
at your favorite retail outlet.

PBAIS